THE DARKNESS

W. J. Lundy

The Darkness

© 2014 W. J. Lundy

Phalanx Press

V2.1.15

Chicago Suburbs

Day of the Darkness, Plus 5

Everything was closed. Jacob's co-workers jokingly called it a FEMA holiday, like a snow day in the summertime. Office buildings were locked up and the government declared a national shutdown with only essential employees required to report. It was rumored that police officers and even medical professionals were starting to walk off the job, refusing to report for duty.

Jacob willingly agreed to working from home until the crisis passed, happy to avoid the traffic for a few days. A long break from all the out-of-town travel would be nice, and he could spend some much-needed family time with his wife and young daughter. As the emergency progressed, internet connections and even the phones began to fail. He tried to call in to the daily meetings at the factory but received a fast busy signal and dead phone lines instead.

Grocery stores sold out of everything as the mass hysteria slowly spread. Gas, milk, eggs, water… everything was hoarded, or the prices raised beyond the average person's reach. By the time Jacob figured out something real was going on, it was too late. He drove by the local superstore and saw armed guards at the entrance of the parking lot. Shoppers were required to show cash before they would be allowed to enter. The store trucks didn't even bother to unload their goods, merchandise being exchanged right out of the backs, like a shady underground marketplace.

The news just seemed so far away and foreign. It was something that happened in the third world, not here in the suburban neighborhoods of Chicago. Jacob sat on his living room sofa, watching a looping satellite broadcast of the chaos in Atlanta. The anchors warned that the rioters had already breached the lobby. Stairwells were piled full of furniture and the elevators sat dead at the bottom of their shafts, but still the rioters came; they destroyed everything in their paths, leaving nothing untouched. Jacob stared at the TV, not knowing what else to do. The loop always stopped at the enraged face of a man with pearly black eyes; the image would freeze before the video re-started.

Jacob turned to watch her pace the room while she dialed the phone over and over, receiving the same steady tone as a response. He knew she was afraid; everyone was. She wanted to go to her parents' home near the lake, north of the city. It was out of town and quiet there; maybe she was right, but how would they get there? Jacob knew the city wouldn't be safe—even the outer areas of Chicago would be chaos—and he couldn't risk it on the interstate, not with Katy. Laura suggested the trains, but that was the last place he wanted to be stranded.

He knew the phones were down, but still she tried, nonetheless. Once she realized she would have no contact with her mother, she would blame him. He knew it was unreasonable but something he would accept if it helped her. Jacob didn't want her to give up on him; he needed her to stay focused. He needed her and Katy to be strong. He couldn't do it alone.

"Give it a couple days, Laura; if nothing changes, we'll try for the city."

Day of the Darkness, Plus 7

"What happened?" Jacob muttered, pulling his head away from the airbag. He tasted blood from a broken lip and smelled oil dripping from a hot motor. Looking over the dash and through a broken windshield, he could see a second vehicle, steam still pouring from its radiator. Jacob could barely hear his daughter, Katy, screaming over the weather siren. In the side mirror, he caught a glimpse of a man in denim dragging his little girl from the car, then lifting her to his chest before turning to run.

Jacob strained and painfully pressed against the driver's door, the metal screeching as he forced it open. Losing his balance, he rolled from the car and onto the street. His daughter's screams faded. He felt anger rising, giving him strength; he scrambled to his feet and ran after the screams. His daughter fought, screaming and flailing her arms and legs, scratching at the man's eyes and nose while struggling. The man dropped her and put his hands to his face, but when he saw Jacob, he turned to lunge. The man's eyes locked on his, and he howled, reaching for him wildly with oily, blood-covered hands.

With his own hands shaking violently, Jacob raised his Ruger P89 pistol and fired quick shots from only feet away; the first rounds went low, the others, directly to the man's chest. Jacob twisted away and dodged as the man's momentum carried him past before the body tumbled to the ground, landing on its stomach. Not waiting to see if he was dead, Jacob turned hard and stepped on the man's back; enraged, he fired one more shot into his head. The body stiffened before going slack. Jacob's terrified daughter screamed from where she lay on the pavement; he scooped her up and ran back to the car.

On the passenger side, Laura was struggling with a second attacker. The large man was on top of her and almost had her pinned to the ground. Jacob sat Katy down, ran full speed, then, leaping onto the man's back, grabbed him under the arms. Rolling forcefully, they tumbled away from Laura and into the grass. The crazed attacker was able to gain position on Jacob. Having the advantage in strength and weight, he tussled and twisted until Jacob found his own back to the ground. The man now stared down into Jacob's face as his hands grasped Jacob's throat and began to squeeze.

Looking into the man's dark eyes, Jacob saw no emotion that could be reasoned with. Like a rabid dog, the man seemed to have no regard for Jacob's life. Jacob pushed against the man's chest and gasped for air while struggling under the attacker's weight. The man suddenly dropped and fell limp over Jacob's chest, having taken a full kick to the side of the head from Laura. Jacob hoisted the body up and rolled it off of him. Grabbing at the grass, he pulled himself away and pushed up into a sitting position. He coughed and choked for oxygen as he looked at the unconscious man. His attention was distracted when he noticed Laura was on the ground, sobbing, and pulling Katy into her lap.

The attacker let out a moan and stretched an arm, reaching for Jacob's ankle. Jacob pawed at the grass until he found the pistol and then turned back to face the man. Leveling the weapon, he shot the attacker once in the face, snapping back its head violently, causing the girls to scream.

Staggering back to his feet, he looked in both directions. Jacob's focused tunnel vision faded enough to allow him to see everything. The sounds of the wailing weather siren seemed to come back even louder than before. It was over. Suddenly exhausted, he struggled to stay on his feet as adrenalin pushed spasms through his legs and knees. Jacob turned and looked around him; his neighbors were standing on their porches, staring at him accusingly. He ignored them and reached down for Laura.

"Are you okay? Come on, get Katy back in the house," he said, lifting Laura to her feet.

Laura looked at him in shock. "What happened?"

"Get Katy back in the house, Laura!" he said over the sound of the siren.

Laura looked at the dead man at her feet. She screamed, "What happened?"

Katy began crying hysterically.

With his heart still racing, he lifted Katy and handed her off to Laura. "Please get her inside; I'll be there in a minute."

Laura turned her head to look at their neighbors before backing away toward the porch. She held Katy's head to her shoulder in a belated attempt to shield the young girl from the horror of what lay on the ground.

He watched them move across the porch and waited for the door to close behind them. Jacob's head ached and the sound of the siren clouded his mind as he struggled to collect his thoughts on what had happened. He stepped to the house and wearily dropped to the porch steps. They were trying to flee to the country, or at least get to Laura's parents north of the city—anywhere as far away from people as they could get. He remembered pulling out of the garage and barely entering the street before the speeding car collided with them. But the men, where did they come from? They must have been pursuing the other car. Why did they attack them?

Under the spiteful eyes of his neighbors, Jacob stood and went to the other car.

"Thanks for the help, guys," he said under his breath.

He ignored their stares and opened the passenger-side door, stretched across the front seat, and checked the man's bloodied wrist for a pulse. The driver was dead; the lack of a seatbelt had allowed his body to partly extend through the windshield.

Looking in the backseat, he found it filled with luggage. He saw a plastic grocery bag stuffed with oranges and bottles of water. Jacob pondered them briefly before taking the bag and joining his wife back in the house. Ignoring his neighbors' cold stares, he shut and locked the house door behind him.

Moving across the room to a window, Jacob parted the curtains and looked into the street. The incessant wailing of the weather siren was better behind the plate-glass window. Even now, with the power out, it wailed. Why had it not been shut off yet? Jacob looked at the smoking vehicles in the street and saw his neighbors approaching.

The anxiety built up in his chest; he was sweating and he felt his heart racing. Jacob was fighting off panic… and losing. He had to do something.

"Laura, get everything and take it upstairs to our bedroom," he said.

Laura was in the kitchen, handing Katy a glass of water, still trying to calm her. "Why? What are we doing?"

"We need to lock ourselves in. I'm afraid they're coming. We need to be ready."

"Those things we saw on the news? Here? Is that what that was?" she asked.

"I don't know. Laura, please… just get all the food and water upstairs. We don't have much time."

Jacob went to the garage and shut the overhead door before retrieving his cordless drill and a box of deck screws. He made a quick pass through his home, locking and bolting every door, closing every curtain.

By habit, he went to arm the alarm by the front door, his fingers nearly touching the buttons. With no power and the backup batteries long dead, the alarm was useless. Jacob shook his head before running up the stairs, taking them two at a time.

Jacob joined his wife at the top, and he followed her into the master suite. Their bedroom was large and square; an antique armoire rested against an interior wall close to the door. A single, long window faced the street, opposite the entrance to the bathroom. A king-sized bed in the center of the room, with a nightstand on each side, filled the rest of the space. Jacob moved to the foot of the bed where Laura had placed everything and took a quick inventory of their belongings. He nodded before turning away to bolt the heavy hardwood bedroom door at the top of the stairs.

Jacob had always been security conscious… or paranoid, as his friends called it. He was on the road a lot for work, and he wanted his family safe when he was away. Laura was against guns and refused to learn to use them, which meant Jacob's firearms were kept in a closet safe when he was away. As a compromise—in Jacob's mind, at least—he'd installed a heavy exterior door at the entrance to their bedroom. The heavy bolt he'd added, to secure it further, effectively turned their master suite into a safe room.

Jacob stopped and looked at the door with the brass bolt lock, talking quietly to himself. "Better than that damn security alarm I spent all the money on," he said. "More practical too, and passive, doesn't require electricity like the alarm. Nothing to train or learn and no fancy monitoring companies… a one-time expense to install, and we have a barrier between us and them…"

He paused when Laura asked, "Who are you talking to?"

Jacob put his hand on the door again and rattled the knob. Checking the lock, he felt the clunk of the steel bolt riding into the two-by-six stud frame.

"Nobody," he said.

Jacob lifted the drill and a handful of screws. He drove the four-inch screws in deep, one in each corner, two in the top, and two on each side.

"What are you doing?" Laura protested. "You're wrecking the door."

Jacob stopped and looked her in the eye. He could see she was in shock and not fully comprehending the situation. She still didn't believe it. In denial, she blocked it out and ignored all of it. Even having felt the violence firsthand, in front of their home, she wasn't getting the urgency of the situation. This wasn't something that happened far away; the violence had reached their front yard. People were killing out there, and nobody was coming to save them. They would have to save themselves.

Laura watched the same news reports he did—the attacks, the disappearances, the mobs, the warnings from police to stay off the streets. At first, they'd compared them to events expected with third-world mentality, like the massacres in the Congo and attacks in Rwanda—even the LA Riots; they simply did not make any sense.

The newscasters relayed messages from mayors urging residents to stay in their homes and wait out the crisis. The government was working on it and the police were organizing a response. The National Guard mobilized and set up evacuation centers. In some cases, though, the evacuation centers were as dangerous as the streets. Several reports aired news of them being wiped out… everyone lost… everyone dead. The warnings were shown on the TV in long, repeating broadcasts before the power went out.

Secured on the second floor, Jacob went to the window and observed the street. The road was wide with tall shade trees on both sides and ran deep into the suburban neighborhood. Well-maintained, cookie-cutter homes sat back from green lawns, interrupted by the destroyed car that was still smoking from the collision just beyond his own driveway. Some of his neighbors had now left their porches and were gathered around it, talking and taking photos with their phones of the dead men.

"What are they doing? Damn it, they need to get inside," Jacob shouted. "The news said to stay in your homes. Did they not see those men? Something is wrong, Laura; they were crazed and couldn't be reasoned with! They need to get back inside!"

Laura went to the window to stand beside him and looked out. "They're doing what you should have done, Jacob! The right thing. You can't just flee the scene—"

"No, it's too dangerous; I don't know what they are. Bath salt nutters, zombies, crazed maniacs… Laura, I'm afraid—"

He was interrupted by a loud, blood-curdling scream from down the street. Jacob strained and focused through the shade of the trees lining the road. A woman was running barefoot toward them and screaming, her ripped clothing covered in blood. She ran directly into a man standing by the wrecked cars. He tried to hold the frantic woman, but she struggled and pointed back down the road. She broke free of the man and continued to scream as she ran away.

Jacob stared in horror when he saw what the woman had pointed at. The mob was just as the newscasters described; they looked crazy and bloodthirsty. Their black eyes stared straight ahead and they shrieked as they filled the street from curb to curb, charging fast like a herd of bulls. He saw the neighbors around the cars begin to scatter while they fled back to their homes. The mobs broke up and splintered to follow them up onto porches and crash through doors.

Jacob grabbed his wife, pulled her to the floor and out of sight, then put a hand over her mouth to muffle her cries. He crawled across the floor with his wife in tow and grabbed his daughter. He brought them both into the en suite bathroom and sat them on the floor, holding them tight and urging them to be quiet.

"What's happening?" Laura sobbed.

"I don't know," Jacob whispered back.

Jacob waited for the noise to stop, the screaming and the pleas for help to fade. He ripped down the shower curtain and, walking low, moved back into the bedroom. He peeked cautiously through the window and saw that the street was clear. The destroyed cars remained, but there was nothing else left. The mob was gone and, with the exception of the dead man still poking through the window, there were no bodies—even the two men he killed were gone. Tattered clothing littered the street and lawns; blood streaks and drag marks showed where victims had been pulled away. The things, whatever they were, seemed to have consumed everything in their path. They recovered their dead and took away the living.

Why leave the man in the car and take the rest? Jacob asked himself.

Searching, he looked at the neighboring houses. Two of them were destroyed, their windows broken and the doors shattered. He then looked at the house across from him. In the second-story window, he could see his neighbor, Smitty, looking back. He waved to Jacob. Jacob returned his gaze and shook his head sadly before stretching the shower curtain across the window to further block out the light.

Chapter 1

A chilling, uncomfortable silence woke him. His wife and daughter lay sleeping beside him, their soft breathing the only noise to reach his ears. Not wanting to move, he opened his eyes and stared at a solitary fly walking across the ceiling. His clothing was soaked with sweat, but he didn't dare remove his heavy shirt and jeans. The room grew hot during the night with the electricity out and the air conditioning along with it. The summer heat and humidity made the space nearly unbearable. Quietly, he worked his way around his daughter, Katy, and pulled his legs to the side of the bed before standing in the blacked-out bedroom.

He was normally a patient man, taking his time to ensure things were done right. He wasn't one to jump to conclusions or make thoughtless decisions—probably why he was good at his job working as a setup engineer. He traveled the country from plant to plant troubleshooting assembly line operations, fixing bottlenecks, and finding solutions to problems. Jacob wasn't hasty in action; he liked to analyze problems and attack them with a well-conceived plan.

Jacob took a deep breath, admonishing himself, warning himself to be cautious—to work out the problem methodically, as he'd always been able to in the past. He reached to the floor at the base of the bed and felt for the jug of water. Finding it, he took a long gulp that quenched his thirst. A cold shower would be better, but that was impossible for now. Why is this happening? For the first time in his life, he didn't have the answers. He wouldn't be able to sketch a solution or logically define the problem. Jacob followed all the rules, did what he was told, and now he felt doomed by it. He feared he had failed his family.

The silence outside was disturbing; he listened intently, feeling his heart beating in his chest and fighting back the steady panic building in his stomach. For nearly a week, the weather siren had wailed day and night without relief. They'd grown accustomed to the whine of the up and down squall blocking out the sounds of the rest of the world. Even after the electrical grid failed, the loud siren blared nonstop. Running off batteries, he presumed, or maybe a generator. None of that mattered now; the siren was off and the night quiet once again. Standing in the center of his bedroom and facing the window, Jacob strained to listen.

He moved closer to the curtains covering the window and finally received the feedback he craved to remind him they were not alone. He heard the barking of a dog in the far distance, a car alarm, a faint scream, and the pop, pop, pop of a firearm. The once quiet neighborhood had slowly become a war zone. Jacob walked to the window and put his fingers to the edge of the heavy drapes.

"Is it over?" He heard Laura whisper from the bed.

Jacob turned and squinted to see her in the dark room. "I don't know; it's quiet—the siren stopped," he answered.

He looked at her as she sat silently on the bed, and he knew she was thinking of her parents north of the city. Jacob thought of the chaos outside and what must be happening far away. What if they had gotten out of the driveway and beyond the neighborhood? The televised backups on the interstates and city streets had made for murderous scenes on the network news channels. Glued to the TV during the first days, Jacob watched the helicopter footage of men being dragged from their cars, police shooting into charging mobs on the magnificent mile, and panicked soldiers running away from their posts.

Jacob moved across the room and sat beside her on the bed. He put his arm around her waist while she rested her head on his shoulder. "Katy isn't speaking," she said.

"I know; I am worried about her too."

Jacob looked back at Katy sleeping peacefully beside them.

"What's happening out there?"

"I think they have it all wrong. The news, they say it started in small towns with crime sprees, and then everyone just went crazy, the entire populations turning to violence overnight."

"It doesn't make any sense. People don't go mad overnight," Laura said.

"I really wasn't that worried until the police started to disappear and they said cops were joining the looters and how after that, it had spread from small towns to the cities. I talked to Jerry at work just a week ago; nobody knows what's going on or how it's spreading so quickly," he said.

"Why don't they just tell us what they want?"

"They don't have a spokesperson and they won't make demands. The President said he was going to implement martial law. You already know they told us to stay home from work, stay at home and off the streets, and they closed schools. I think the government knows more than they are telling us."

Laura sat up taller, looking at him. "Jenny said she heard it all has something to do with the meteor shower last weekend, like maybe it polluted the water, and it's making people crazy. Smitty says they weren't meteors at all; he said it was a signal, like a sign."

"Smitty is a tool; a sign for what?" Jacob asked, already having a low opinion of his neighbor.

"Well, Smitty says the Chinese or North Korean sleeper cells have probably been activated to disrupt the economy."

"Ha! What economy?" Jacob asked.

"Well then, maybe it's global warming; or like Jenny said, something in the water or chemicals in the food. All those people on the TV, the experts, they all seemed to have an opinion—at least they did until the experts began to vanish too."

Jacob sat and, listening to her, he second-guessed his earlier inaction. Maybe if they'd left at the first signs of danger, they wouldn't be trapped here. They would be safe at Laura's parents in the country. Now they were stuck, left alone to starve… or worse.

"I think you were right, Laura; we should have left when we had the chance."

"It's okay. You were just trying to keep us safe. You did what you thought was right," she said.

Jacob stood and stepped closer to the window, then pulled back on the edge of the drape, letting the bright moonlight bleed into the room. He put his eye to the crack; the skies were clear and the moon hung full, casting a blue hue over the residential street and turning the pavement a gloomy shade of gray. On the horizon, the skyline glowed orange and yellow.

He could see his wrecked car in the center of the road where they'd abandoned it. The car that hit him was twisted, the body of the driver still hanging from the windshield. Jacob tried to look away, but the wreckage mesmerized him. Every time he looked at it, his eyes were drawn back to the body… the man's bloated corpse mangled by the glass… the oily stains on the sidewalk where the other bodies had been…

Movement caught his eye. Jacob instinctively crouched and backed away, even though he didn't think anyone would be able to see him peeking from the darkened second story window.

"What is it? Did you see something?" Laura whispered.

In a low crouch, Jacob went back to the window and scanned the street. There, against a curb, stood a shirtless man, his naked arms tensed, his head locked straight ahead in a dark stare. Standing like a stone at the edge of the street, the man didn't move.

Jacob heard the squeak and rattle of a storm door. He concentrated on trying to find the source of the noise and pushed closer to the gap in the drapes.

"No. What are you doing?" he whispered, as he caught a glimpse of his neighbor's front door slowly opening.

The door squeaked and pushed out. A man dressed in khaki pants and a heavy robe walked onto the porch. Smitty, his neighbor of five years, stepped into the moonlight with an aluminum baseball bat held loosely in his right hand. He pointed the bat with an extended arm and called out.

"Hey... hey you! Why'd the siren go out?" Smitty said to the stranger in the street.

The bare-chested man turned his head to look at him. His arms flexed and extended, pointing at Smitty. His back arched and he let out a yell—no words, just an anger-filled roar. Jacob watched his neighbor take a step back in fear.

All along the street, more figures came into view from the shadows. They were running at full speed, screaming. They poured past the bare-chested man and ran to the house. Smitty ran inside and closed the door just as the mob crashed into the front of the home. The wood siding rattled and the windows buckled from the impact. Jacob watched as they piled over the porch, surrounding the perimeter of the home, searching for away in while tearing at the windows and siding.

The mob exploded through the front windows and crashed through the door. They continued to pour down the street—at least a hundred of them—all entering Smitty's home. There were no screams from inside the house. No cries for help. Nothing could be heard over the roar of the ravenous mob. Jacob let go of the drape, rolled away, and pressed his back to the wall. The thunder of his neighbor's home being torn apart shook his own and he barely heard his daughter's cry from the bed.

His wife pulled her close, whispering as she tried to comfort the girl. Jacob went to the nightstand, gripped his pistol, and walked to the bedroom door. He checked the locks, feeling the long wood screws he had fastened into the doorframe. "What's happening outside, Jacob?" his wife asked.

"I don't know," he answered. He searched the floor and lifted the water jug to his lips and then mumbled, "They're attacking Smitty's house."

"What? Jenny and the kids!" Laura said as she jumped to her feet and began running to the window.

Jacob moved quickly to stop her; he didn't want her to see. He didn't want her to make a commotion that could be detected from the street. He pushed her away and back to the bed.

"More of the rioters?" she asked as she turned away from him.

"They are not rioters; just be quiet... please. They'll hear us."

The sound of the mob slowly dissipated and Jacob worked up the courage to return to the window. When he looked out, the mob was gone, the bare-chested man along with them. His neighbor's home was destroyed. Windows were shattered, the door was gone, the walls splintered, and much of the front porch had collapsed.

With no sign of anyone, the area was once again quiet. The previous mayhem on the street had retreated back into the shadows with the mob, leaving Smitty's once quaint and well-maintained home destroyed. Jacob searched the neighboring properties and found many in the same condition. Nearly every other house showed signs of attack.

How long before they come for us? Jacob thought.

He moved to the foot of the bed and sat on the floor. The rifle that leaned against the wooden bed frame near his head wasn't much; a squirrel gun, his dad called it. It was a .22LR—magazine fed and reliable, but not much stopping power. He should have bought a larger rifle when he'd had a chance, and he'd had plenty, stopping to look at them on trips to the outdoor stores, admiring the stealthy look of the exotic assault rifles. He always wanted one, but Jacob wasn't a hunter and he didn't spend weekends at the range, so how would he have justified the purchase?

An inherited handgun passed down from his father for home defense and the rifle he kept from his childhood seemed to be plenty enough at the time.

A nearby gunshot shocked him back into the present. He resisted the temptation to go to the window this time. There was no reason to look; he wouldn't be going to anyone's aid. There would be no opportunity for escape. If anything, he would reveal himself and those things—those monsters—would make their way into his home. If they came for his family, he wouldn't be able to stop them. No, he wouldn't look. Instead, he sat at the edge of the bed, listening to the screams and praying that the weather siren would come back on.

Jacob took another sip of the water, careful to ration it. He'd filled the bathtub of the adjoining master bathroom while the water was still running, just like the news people advised. He knew he could use it to refill the bottles, but it hadn't come to that yet. More gunshots rang out, even closer now; he heard his daughter whimper at the sound of each noise. He could hear yelling now, followed by footfalls in the streets. A man was running, but Jacob still refused to go to the window. He wouldn't get involved and put his family at risk.

"What are we doing? Do we just wait for them to come for us too?" his wife whispered. "Wait for them to kill us or take us away… one at a time?"

"What do you suggest? Want us to go out there on the street? You know what happened last time," he said, pointing at the window.

"I don't know… anything, Jacob. I just can't stay here anymore. Not like this. Katy's sick; I think she needs a doctor," she whispered.

Katy hadn't spoken since the attack on the street. He thought it was shock, but she refused to eat or drink and now she had a fever. Jacob got to his feet and walked along the side of the bed. "Wait till morning; we'll figure out a way. We will get out of here," he whispered.

Jacob turned away from her and walked into the attached bathroom. A small window was positioned high on the wall at the end of the room. Days earlier, Jacob had covered the window with a piece of cardboard. He carefully peeled back the material and looked into the backyard. Dark, quiet, and no movement, but in the distance he could see the yellows and oranges of a new day beginning.

He moved and took a seat on a stool near the bathroom vanity. He smiled, thinking how he'd walked past this stool thousands of times, but never sat on it. He'd put it in here for his daughter; his wife would brush her hair here every morning. Jacob never bothered to admire the stool and how high it sat, how uncomfortable it was. Now it was the only chair in this part of the house.

Looking in the mirror at the bruise on his face from the airbag, the purple swelling under his eyes, he thought back to the previous day—the day of the accident… the look of hate on their faces… the dark, soulless eyes of the attackers…

Laura whispering to Katy in the bedroom brought him out of his trance. He looked up from the stool and deep into his reflection in the vanity mirror. His face was stubbled. His hair was matted. Three days of holding out in the upstairs of their home, with no showers and using a bucket as a toilet, told him they would have to make plans soon. They couldn't stay here indefinitely.

After 9/11, Jacob researched and studied survival. Although he didn't become a prepper or do anything drastic, he wanted to be educated. Shelter in place, food and water for three days, hold out, and help will come was the common mantra. Jacob did his part, but help wasn't here. Where were they? Why hadn't the police knocked on their doors or the Red Cross arrived with food and water? He feared they would never come.

Jacob moved back to the bedroom. His wife was opening a package of crackers to feed their daughter. She looked up at him disapprovingly.

"What?" he said.

"Why are we still here?" she asked. "This is the last of the crackers. Then what?"

"Are you serious? Were you not around yesterday when we tried to leave? Or when I killed those men to get us back into the house?"

"We should have kept going," she said. "Walked, ran... whatever we had to do."

"Oh my god, you're impossible!" he said.

Frustrated, Jacob walked to the far end of the room and sat at the head of the bed. He grabbed the small battery-operated radio and clicked it on. There was static on all stations but one—a local AM frequency that had been broadcasting the same emergency message for the past forty-eight hours. The same useless garbage—stay off the streets, help will come; shelter in place; if you must evacuate, go to the park. Jacob shook his head and shut the radio off before tossing it to the bed.

His wife looked up at him. "We should do it. We should go to the park."

"That message is days old; how do we even know anyone will be there?"

She looked at him while biting her lip. "I want to leave. I will go without you!" she said.

"It's going to be okay, Laura."

He knew she wouldn't leave; she wouldn't go without him. He got the message though. It was time for them to go, but at what cost? Why leave this piece of shelter for the open streets? Jacob got up from the bed and helped his wife pack items into the bag. Although it seemed that it calmed her nerves, when she looked at him he could see she was holding back tears.

"I know," he said, touching her cheek. "I'll keep you safe. I promise."

"How? What if they find us?" she sobbed.

Jacob held her and looked at his daughter on the bed. "I don't know; they just can't."

Chapter 2

With late afternoon, came the sweltering heat. Jacob pulled the drapes away from the window to try to allow a draft, but only hot air entered. He paced through the room, sweating. He wanted to go downstairs and sit in the family room or venture into the basement den where it was always cool. His wife was sitting on the bathroom floor, fanning herself, when Jacob walked past her and entered the walk-in closet adjacent to the room. He looked up at the ceiling and thought about the attic. He knew it would be just as hot, but it was also vented and with the window in the gable end, he'd have a better view of the street.

The attic access was in the hallway outside the sealed bedroom door. Not wanting to compromise their security, he decided he would just make a new entrance. Jacob retrieved a knife from his nightstand and climbed the tall shelves to the ceiling of the closet. He jabbed the blade of the knife into the sheet rock. Dust and bits of insulation poured down over his face and shoulders. He squinted to protect his eyes and worked until he'd created a fist-sized hole. He then stuck his hand in and broke away at it until he'd created a large opening between the ceiling joists.

With a hole large enough to enter the attic, Jacob stuck his head through and pushed away the rolled bats of insulation. Looking in all directions, he could see little; the attic was dark with only small bits of dust-filled light entering through the vent. He dropped back down and called for his wife. When she entered the room below, she looked at his body partway into the destroyed ceiling, then looked up at him with her hand held over her mouth, and eyes wide. "What are you doing?"

"Get me the flashlight," he said, not answering her question.

"Why? You're not going up there," she argued.

"Just get me the light, Laura," he said as patiently as he could.

He heard rustling below him and looked down to see that she'd climbed the shelf partway to meet him. She passed up the light. Jacob took it, clicked it on, and then pulled himself into the attic. He crawled across the joists to a center portion, floored with plywood and filled with holiday decorations. He heard a noise by the hole and saw his wife's head looking back at him.

"Why are you up here?" she asked again.

Jacob crawled to the gable that was above their bedroom. Seated in the end was a large louvered vent cap; it was normally pushed open by a thermostat-controlled electric fan. The surface of the fan was enclosed in a cage and full of louvers that were currently closed. "I wanted to see if I could get some air flowing," he said back to her.

Jacob pushed his hands against the electric motor and found it firmly in place, blocking the gable vent. He forced the knife blade into the mounting screws, trying to break them free but failing. Behind him, Laura dropped below, then quickly returned before reaching out to pass Jacob his drill. He smiled as he took it from her and then, working carefully, he was able to remove the bracket and drop the fan motor to the floor. After working at one of the exposed vents with his knife, he felt it give as the plastic louver broke free and snapped off. He repeated this with two more of the louvers and was quickly rewarded with a slight drawing of the attic air.

He looked back at his wife and could see her hair gently flowing up as cooler air from downstairs was pulled through the master suite and out of the attic window, the natural rise of the hot air creating a draft. The temperature decrease was subtle, but the moving air across their skin felt like heaven after sweltering in the sealed room.

She smiled at him approvingly. Jacob moved his eye closer to the vent, looking through the gap created from the broken louvers. He pressed close and looked in all directions. Far in the distance, he could see billowing smoke from fires and abandoned cars at intersections. The streets were void of all traffic. Intersections that were normally busy stood silent with debris in the streets.

Houses that still stood were closed up tight and had their window blinds closed. With cars visible in some driveways, he knew people were still around;

they had to be. Everyone couldn't be gone. The smart ones that followed the instructions, they were inside hiding the same as we are. They had to be, Jacob thought as he sat watching and listening. He heard his wife crawl up behind him, and she pressed close. Jacob eased out of the way so she could look through the louvers. He watched her jaw drop as she gasped over the scene of their small bit of neighborhood.

"Oh my God. Jacob, this is really happening, isn't it?" she croaked.

He put his hand on the back of her neck, not speaking. She looked at him. "What are we going to do, Jacob?"

"We just need to hold on."

She backed away from the gable vent and sat silently. A muffled cry from below caught her attention and Laura turned to look at the access hole. "I'll check on her; don't be too long," she whispered as she crawled away.

He turned back to follow her to the master suite. Moving across the attic, he paused and looked at the plywood floor filled with plastic bins and boxes. He pushed them aside and made his way to the pulldown attic access ladder. He found a long board and slid it through the handle, locking it into the up position. Jacob turned and moved back to the makeshift hole and, grabbing the joists, lowered himself back onto the closet shelving.

He found Laura scooping a small paper cup of water from the bathtub. She used it to wet her hands, then wiped them down the sides of Katy's cheeks. She looked up at Jacob and said, "She's burning up. I'm not sure what it is, but we're going to need real food; all that's left are some scraps, nothing solid."

Jacob bit his lip, knowing she was right. He could see Katy needed a doctor; he nodded his head. He stood in front of her, and, although he was listening, he was thinking about their supplies. They'd used the last cans of soup already, having eaten it cold, and the fruit was gone the day before. As their luck would have it, everything had happened on the day before grocery day when the cupboards were already bare. He could check the kitchen again, look for something they may have missed in the pantry, but it wasn't likely there would be anything there. Jacob walked through the bathroom and again stood by the bedroom window. He pulled back the drapes and peered across the street.

Smitty's house was a shattered mess after the mob had attacked a few hours ago, but maybe something was left—a scrap of food in the kitchen or something. The house was directly across the street; if he moved quickly, he could cross without being seen. As if agreeing with someone, he nodded his head and moved to his dresser. He pulled out a black, hooded sweatshirt and a pair of dark jeans. He searched a desk drawer and removed a small paddle holster for his handgun. After pulling on his jeans and tucking the holster into his pants over his hip, he dropped in the Ruger pistol until it clicked into place.

"What are you doing now?" Laura asked.

Jacob quickly dressed in the rest of the new attire and dumped one of the backpacks they'd previously packed full of their clothing. "I'm going over to Smitty's to see if there's anything left."

"What? No, it isn't safe; their house was attacked, Jacob," Laura protested.

"Maybe that's what will make it safe. They might not come back to it."

"What if they do?"

Jacob pulled the backpack over his shoulders. He removed and checked the slide of his handgun, dropped the magazine to make sure it was full, and then placed a spare in a small pocket at the front of the holster. He grabbed a black ball cap from atop the armoire, then looked back at Laura. "You said it yourself. She needs real food." Jacob picked up the drill, walked to the bedroom door, and stood there staring at the screws.

"How do you know they'll have anything?" Laura asked.

"I don't Laura, but I have to try."

Shaking his head slightly, Jacob set the drill down next to the door and walked through the bathroom and back to the closet to look up at the hole in the ceiling. "Listen, if I come up empty, I'll try another place, but that's it. Then I'll come back, okay? I won't stay out long; you can watch me from the window."

He snugged the straps on his backpack, then turned to hug her before he grabbed the shelves and pulled himself back into the attic.

Jacob asked Laura to follow him as he worked his way back to the ladder hatch. He showed her how he removed the board securing it, and then lowered the ladder into the hallway below. Looking down, he saw nothing out of the ordinary. He kissed Laura on the cheek and told her to pull up and secure the ladder behind him. She nodded reluctantly.

When he poked his head out of the hatch, he could make out the stairway leading to the first floor. Jacob slowly descended the ladder and stood in the hallway outside of his bedroom door. He folded the attic ladder and let it ride back to the up position. Jacob drew his pistol and slowly approached the stairs.

The rooms below were dark, the heavy drapes still in place. He crept down the stairs and entered the living room where he pulled back the curtains slightly and surveyed the front yard. Empty—nothing in sight. Jacob approached the front door; then, having second thoughts, he walked to the kitchen and used a side door to enter the attached garage. Going through the garage, he could exit out onto the back deck and sneak around to the side yard while staying hidden from view.

Jacob opened the deadbolt on the utility door leading to the garage. He paused in the doorway listening before cautiously entering. He then locked the door behind him, placed the key in his pocket, and began to creep through the dark garage. The stall where the family car usually sat was empty—a grim reminder of the danger he faced. He moved to the back and quietly opened the door leading to the deck. A quick look in both directions and he moved outside, silently pulling the door closed behind him.

He crouched low and hid behind the unkempt, overgrown evergreen bushes. Jacob was thankful that he'd failed to trim them for several years. He dropped to his hands and knees and followed the perimeter of his house until he'd entered the side yard. A tall wooden fence divided his yard from that of his neighbors, the Johnsons. He hadn't seen or heard from them in days, but their home was still secure. They had either left or were locked up tight, the same as he was. He considered going to their door and asking for help, but more people would add complications; not to mention, they might turn him away—or worse, attract attention.

"No, stick to the plan," he whispered to himself as he moved to the front corner of his house. He could see Smitty's driveway. His beaten and battered Lexus still sat parked in front of the garage. Smitty was always an arrogant prick and not someone Jacob would call a friend. He knew the garage would be empty; Smitty parked the Lexus on the street so people would see it. He considered it a status symbol. Now it was a dented wreck with broken windows. Bits of the car's glass lay covering the driveway, reflecting the sunlight.

Crouched at the front corner of his own porch, Jacob eased his head out of the bushes and searched in both directions for movement. It appeared clear. He took one more deep breath and took off at a dead run, flying through his front yard, across the street, up the driveway, and past the Lexus to the garage door that was pushed inward and broken. Jacob knew all the houses on the block had a similar layout with a door leading to the kitchen from the garage, and Smitty's would be no exception. He quickly ducked down and crawled through the broken hole in the overhead garage door. Catching his breath, he crept into the darkness and pressed his back against the wall.

Looking back into the street, things were still as quiet as he'd left them. He looked up at the second story of his own house, just barely detecting movement of the drapes in his master bedroom. Even though he couldn't see her, he knew Laura was watching. He flashed a quick thumbs up, then turned, and ducked deeper into the garage. Jacob stepped over a dumped cabinet of oil and paint cans, then around scattered toolboxes. He rummaged through tools, searching for weapons or anything useful, taking note of things he may need later before finally making it to the small set of steps that led to the open kitchen door.

He paused at the landing to listen, hearing only the rattle of window blinds blowing in the breeze as they scraped and scratched against the shards of broken glass left hanging in their frames. The house smelled dusty and earthy from the opened walls. Jacob took a silent step and peered into the kitchen.

Looking straight through the long kitchen into the house, he could see into the dining room where the eight-seat mahogany furniture set was shattered and crushed into pieces. To the left and right, cupboards were knocked off the walls. The refrigerator was knocked from its place and lying across the floor. Slowly, Jacob moved forward and hid behind an L-shaped counter on the right that divided the kitchen from a family room with a small bar. He took light steps deeper into the kitchen and looked through the bar window into the family room. Focusing beyond upended leather furniture, he could see the home's heavy oak front door had been ripped from its hinges and shredded like balsa wood.

Jacob looked behind him in the direction of a stairwell and saw the body. The man's naked legs twisted back to creep out from behind the railing. One foot was turned out, still wearing a black slipper. Unable to stop himself, he crept forward on the balls of his feet. He paused just in front of the stairs and looked down at Smitty's broken form. His head was pulled as if dislocated from his shoulders, only hanging on by stretched and discolored skin. His left shoulder was green and grotesque, yet Smitty's right hand still clutched a bloodied aluminum bat. Looking closer, Jacob could see bits of hair and fat sticking to the dented end.

"You fought hard," Jacob said.

Suddenly repulsed, Jacob raced away and dry-heaved into a corner of the room. He wiped his watery eyes before staggering back toward the kitchen. Losing his balance on debris, he nearly fell but put a hand on the kitchen counter and took deep breaths to try to calm himself. He relaxed and dropped into a crouched position. Looking across the room, he spotted a large, red camper cooler. Jacob crawled through the space on all fours and popped open the lid.

There wasn't much inside, three bottles of sports drink and half a cooler full of water from melted ice, but he was happy to have it. Jacob quickly dropped the full bottles into his bag, then looked around the kitchen for an empty jug. He dumped over a blue recycling bin against the wall, then rummaged through it and found an old water jug. Jacob opened it and filled the jug with the water from the cooler. If he had to, he could boil the water for drinking if he managed to build a fire, or, at the least, he could use it for bathing. He searched the kitchen, carefully stepping over bits of broken glass while trying to remain quiet. In a crushed cabinet, he found a half box of instant oatmeal, some canned sardines, several cans of soup, and a jar of bouillon cubes—his hope was renewed.

Chapter 3

Jacob looked into his pack one last time, taking inventory of his meager finds, before he glanced back at Smitty's corpse. "It's not much, but thank you," he whispered.

He pulled the sides of the bag tight and zipped the backpack shut. Turning toward the garage, Jacob froze as he found himself standing a mere feet away from a young girl. She was alone, in the doorway of the kitchen. She was missing a shoe and dressed in soiled jeans and a torn top. Jacob methodically dropped his hand from the shoulder strap of the backpack and let it find the grip of his still holstered pistol. He held his breath while trying to search beyond the girl and into the garage to see if she was alone. She looked familiar, but he knew she wasn't part of Smitty's family. She was looking away as if in a faraway place—not speaking, just staring into the floor space where a refrigerator had been before it was knocked to the floor.

She took a soft step in the direction of Jacob, still looking down at the floor. She moved deliberately, like an animal; her feet plodded up and down, arms twitching as her neck stretched, examining the void between the cabinets.

Jacob's hand caressed the grip of the pistol; he squeezed it with his sweaty palm and let his finger drop straight over the receiver. He swallowed hard and in a low voice he asked her, "Are you okay?"

The girl's pale head snapped up to face Jacob; her eyes were a deep, solid black. When she opened her mouth, it revealed glossy white teeth wrapped in dark-purple gums. Her mouth stretched wide, her bottom jaw quivered, and she went to scream just as the sound of a gunshot filled the air. The girl's head twitched and twisted toward the garage, like that of cat quickly searching for prey.

Jacob didn't hesitate; he drew the pistol in a smooth motion and fired a single round into the girl's chest. He saw that where the bullet punched through the girl's light cotton top, black, oozing blood slowly filled the fabric. For a brief moment, Jacob feared he'd made a terrible mistake. His empty left hand reached out to help her, feeling regret for his actions.

The girl's eyes looked back at him with hate. She hissed, letting the last of the air escape her body before she fell back to the ground. Jacob lunged forward and bolted past her for the door. He heard another series of gunshots and, recognizing the sounds of his .22 rifle, he stumbled his way through the garage, and then charged headlong into the driveway.

A teenage boy dressed in a T-shirt and jeans was searching the sky for the source of the gunfire as rounds skipped off the asphalt and smacked into the Lexus. Jacob looked toward the second story of his house and saw the shiny, blued barrel of the rifle poking out, accompanied by silver puffs of smoke wafting from the muzzle. The boy halted in place upon discovering Jacob. Its body turned in his direction and charged without warning as its mouth unhinged inhumanly wide, its black eyes showing no mercy.

Jacob raised the pistol and fired as fast as his finger would allow. Multiple rounds scored several hits as the thing collided with him and knocked him to the asphalt. Anticipating the impact, Jacob rolled back and went with it, then flung the now dead boy off of him. He continued rolling until he was on all fours. Not wasting time to look, he scrambled on his hands and knees onto the lawn, pulled himself to his feet, and bolted across the yard and into the street.

He didn't stop. Fleeing what was behind him, he ran for the side yard of his house and dove into thick bushes that scratched his face and cut into his hands while he clawed his way into the cover of the foliage. When it was too tight to crawl, he dropped to his belly and dragged himself ahead until he was tight against the foundation of the house. Jacob burrowed in and buried his face into the soft dirt. Clenching his eyes tight and trying to control his breathing, he lay there, listening but struggled to hear anything above the beating of his own heart. Jacob pulled himself into a more open space near the wall and rolled over to face the street. Seeing nothing, he attempted to stand, but then he heard footsteps. He froze, and letting his body go limp, he dropped back to the ground where he again tried to become one with the earth. The gunfire had halted, and Jacob prayed his wife was wise enough to return to her hiding place.

He cautiously lifted his head and laid his ear to the earth so that he could see the road. Several people were walking the street and scouring the area; their heads shifted from side to side as they searched for him. He watched as they left the street and surrounded the boy in the driveway. One lifted the dead thing and cradled it in his arms. With no emotion, it turned around and left, carrying the boy. Shortly afterwards, another left the confines of the house carrying the girl.

Why take them and leave Smitty? Jacob asked himself.

The Others loitered in the area for several minutes, not actively searching but clustered in the center of the street, as if they didn't know what to do without direction. They moved to the edges of the street, standing near the curb looking out, their eyes watching the surrounding houses. Jacob heard no communication between them, no whispering, no orders, or commands; nobody seemed to be in charge. Eventually, they stopped moving altogether and stood motionless, frozen in the street.

Jacob lay with his head in the soil, afraid to move. He could feel insects crawl across his neck, and leaves tickled his nose, but he didn't dare move for fear that he'd alert the black-eyed things standing in the center of the street. Gunshots sounded far in the distance followed by a woman's scream; the things' heads lifted all at once as if a switch powered them on. In unison, they turned and took off in the direction of the sound. Soon after, Jacob heard the high-pitched wail that he knew was their call, followed by the rumble of an attack. He crawled along the perimeter of the house until he was clear of the bushes, then scrambled for his garage door.

He made it inside then closed and bolted the door shut mere moments before losing his stomach onto the cement floor. His eyes watered as he gagged and coughed while pacing the room. He stopped beside the small steps leading to his house; he sat there collecting himself, but when he went to wipe his face with the sleeve of his hoodie, he noticed the boy's blood. He looked down and saw it was on his hands and clothing. It clung to his fingers. It wasn't red or sticky, or anything at all like he would expect the texture of human blood to be. He quickly pulled off the black hoodie and tossed it to the center of the room. He looked at his hands and saw that the black, greasy stains were still on his fingers.

Jacob grabbed a rag from a workbench and scrubbed his hands with a bottle of solvent. The greasy blood clung to his skin and tingled. He used the rag and scrubbed at his palms; the blood finally came off as a single rubber-like glob that then curled back on itself. With disgust, he let it drop to the floor. Jacob's curiosity peaked and he quickly retrieved the sweatshirt. He looked at the rest of the bloodstains, watching them shrink and retract like a heavy rubber film that was dry rotting as he watched. After a couple minutes, he was able to grab it by the edge and completely remove it from the sweatshirt. He lifted it and dropped it to the floor where it changed from the greasy black to an ashen gray.

"What the hell?" he muttered as he scuffed the remaining traces of it away with the toe of his boot. "What is this stuff?"

He dug through his pocket for his keys and re-entered his home. He wanted nothing more than to collapse into the comfy sofa in the far room and pretend everything was back to normal. Jacob shook away the thoughts, knowing Laura and Katy would be anxious after watching him disappear and not knowing where he went. Jacob dragged his tired legs up the stairs and pulled down the attic ladder in a pre-arranged knock. After a moment, he heard the board slide away and when the ladder dropped, he saw his wife looking down at him over the sights of the rifle.

"I thought I'd never see you again," she said quietly.

Jacob nodded and quickly climbed the ladder, pulling it up behind him and barricading it. He reached out for her while still in the attic, grabbing her hands then embracing her in a tight hug.

She looked up at him. "I'm sorry I shot the gun... I didn't know what else to do—its eyes... they were so black," she cried.

Hugging her and trying to calm her, he said, "I know... You did the right thing, Laura. There was another one inside; I might not have gotten away if you hadn't fired."

They sat silently in the attic until Jacob removed the backpack and indicated for Laura to lead the way back into the rooms below. They moved into the bathroom and sat on the floor, leaning against the tub while he dumped the contents of the bag and separated the sports drinks. "It's not a lot, but we can drink water and save these for Katy. They'll help with her dehydration; at least until her fever drops."

Laura picked up the items, sorting them into piles. "She still isn't speaking," Laura whispered. "I'm scared."

"I know; so am I. It has to just be the stress. She has been through a lot," Jacob said. "She'll be okay once we get out of here and to some place safe. We just need to care for her and make her comfortable until then."

Laura nodded her head in agreement and tried to hide her tears. She wiped her eyes with the sleeve of her blouse then opened one of the drinks, poured the liquid into a small sippy cup, and left the bathroom. Jacob followed her out and while Laura helped the girl drink, Jacob walked to the bedroom window. He saw the rifle propped against the wall and looked down at the brass shell casings littering the carpet. Jacob removed the magazine and locked back the bolt, removing a round. He grabbed a yellow box from his nightstand, reloaded, and charged the weapon before leaning it back against the wall.

"What are they?" Laura whispered, not looking up from her task at hand. "Those weren't kids down there."

Jacob walked away from the window and sat on the bed, reloading his pistol. "I don't know. The girl… she looked familiar, but when I spoke to her… her eyes… and the way she reacted to me. I didn't even hear her until she was right behind me."

"I don't know where they came from. I was watching the street and then all of a sudden, they were there. I watched the girl go into the house. I wanted to warn you… I didn't know how. The boy—that was the Emersons' son. His little sister, Mia, used to ride Katy's bus. He looked up at us and I know he couldn't see me, but through the scope—I saw his eyes, Jacob, they were so dark, like there was nothing behind them, and then his head darted to the house, like he heard you. I was so scared… I fired; I didn't know what else to do. I shot him, Jacob!" she said, holding back tears.

"It's okay. You did good, Laura. It's okay."

"Was it Mia? The girl, was it her?" Laura asked hesitantly.

"Not anymore; I don't know what she was."

"Did she attack you?"

"She would have. I'm certain of it," he mumbled.

"I heard your gun. Did you kill her?"

"I don't know; I watched them take her away."

Jacob sat down wearily. "I found some soup," he said, changing the subject. "You should eat."

"You haven't eaten, Jacob."

He lay back on the bed, closing his eyes. "I'm okay… I just want to rest," he said.

Chapter 4

"Jacob, Jacob, wake up," Laura whispered.

He turned over and looked at the dark ceiling, searching the room in a daze. It was early in the evening; the sun was just beginning to go down and low light still broke the edge of the curtains. Katy was sleeping soundly at the foot of the bed. Jacob closed his eyes tightly, then opened them again, blinking until his vision cleared. He looked at Laura lying next to him. "What is it?" he asked, still groggy.

"Someone is—" she began as a cracking of wood sounded from somewhere outside behind their house.

Jacob froze and put his hand to her lips. He rolled out of the bed and placed his feet on the floor as his right hand searched the nightstand for his pistol. He felt its cool frame and gripped it tight. There was another bang and a thump from somewhere outside. He got up and crept around the foot of the bed and walked to the bathroom window. He slowly pulled back the cardboard and looked into the yard.

Two crouched figures were next to the plank wood fence that separated his yard from his neighbors. They were young—teens, maybe early twenties—wearing light backpacks. One, a young man, held a crowbar; a young girl was close behind him. They were looking in the direction of his back deck. There was another sound of splitting wood followed by a loud pop, and he saw the two individuals get to their feet and run to the deck.

Jacob knew someone was breaking in and that they'd managed to jimmy open the French doors off the family room. He heard them below now as they closed the door. Muffled voices seemed to direct someone to move furniture—probably to brace the destroyed door. Jacob looked behind him and saw his wife through the open bathroom door, sitting up in the bed with Katy in her lap. He held a finger to his lips as he crept toward her and stopped to kneel next to a heat register in the floor. With his ear pressed against it, the ductwork funneled the muffled sounds from below.

"There isn't shit here. Why are we stopping, Frank?" a young male voice said.

"We need to hold up, at least until morning. We can't keep stumbling around in the dark; they'll find us," answered a gruff older man's voice.

Jacob listened to the two males arguing, the female remaining silent. The sound of kitchen cabinets and the pantry doors opening and closing were followed by complaints about the house having no food or water. He listened as they continued to stomp through the house, opening and dumping drawers… then a foot fell on the bottom steps.

Jacob took his ear from the floor vent and, returning to the bedroom, moved to his wife's side to scoop up his daughter. He kept her head against his chest in case she made a sound. Jacob quickly moved them through the bathroom and into the walk-in closet. Laura sat in a corner, and Jacob placed Katy in her lap. He told his wife to be silent and wait for him. As he crept back, she reached out and grabbed his arm.

"What are you going to do?" she whispered.

"Let's just see who they are first," he said, walking into the bedroom. He took a position where he could observe the heavy wooden door.

The steps slapped against the hardwood stair treads. Whoever was attached to the feet was not trying to be quiet. The footfalls sounded thunderous over the silence of the room, and Jacob imagined heavy work boots. The sound dulled as the feet left the stair treads and stepped onto the carpet at the top. He heard them near the door. He stared intently at the knob and watched it turn side to side. Then it rattled as someone shook the handle, the heavy door hardly budging thanks to being locked tightly in place with the screws.

"Hey, Joey! We got a locked door up here!" the gruff voice called out.

"Will you be quiet?" Jacob heard another respond. "You want them to hear us?"

The door rattled again. "Boy, they ain't going to hear us indoors."

Jacob heard softer footsteps running up the treads, followed by a second set. The lighter footsteps approached the door and Jacob could hear them shuffling around on the landing. The knob turned and rattled again.

"Damn, who puts a bolt lock on an inside door?" the younger voice muttered.

Jacob heard metal slide along the doorframe then a creak and pop of splintering wood. He knew one of them was applying a crowbar to the doorjamb. He ducked into the bathroom doorway and leaned out, keeping the pistol in his hand. He was confident the door wouldn't move with the deck screws. Even if they were able to seat the crow bar, they would need a fire axe to remove it from its frame.

"Wait, there might be people in there; let's just leave it alone." Jacob heard the girl speak for the first time.

"Girl, you're stu—"

"Damn it, Frank, I told you not to talk to her like that," the younger man said.

An exaggerated laugh echoed in the hallway. "Boy, what are you going to do about it? You'd be dead right now if I hadn't come back for your ass."

"Screw you, Frank; we were getting along just fine without you," the girl said.

"The hell you were. Now shut up before I slap you both upside the head with this bar," the gruff voice said laughing.

There was another clunk as the bar pried into the doorframe, causing a slight creaking of wood, then the bar popped and the man yelped. "Dammit; smashed my knuckles!" he shouted.

The man huffed and breathed hard until, suddenly, a thud resonated as the man punched the door.

"This fucker is solid," Frank said. "Maybe we can get some tools in the morning and try again."

Jacob heard the crowbar drop to the carpet.

"Or… maybe I should just shoot the lock."

"Are you crazy? They'll hear that for sure," the girl argued.

"Boy, you better shut that little bitch up before I do," Frank said.

There was a commotion on the landing that sounded like fists being thrown. Heavy breathing and grunting were accompanied by banging against the door as something hard smacked against it over and over again.

"Stop, Frank! You'll kill him," pleaded the girl. The banging against the door stopped, then Jacob heard a loud slap and the girl whimpered. "This is your fault. If you'd just kept your mouth shut!" Frank yelled. "Take this piece of shit downstairs before I kick both your asses. I should have never come back for you," he said, grunting and breathing heavy.

Jacob could hear the soft steps fade as they fumbled down the stairs. The other man's heavy breathing remained. He thudded against the door, and Jacob could hear him slide down to the floor. He was muttering to himself. The sound of a lighter sparked to life and soon after, Jacob could smell cigarette smoke as it drifted through the cold air return.

He knew the man was lying against the door. He could easily muffle the gun with a pillow and press it against the wood; a single shot is all it would take, if he guessed correctly. A quick shot in the night. The people downstairs would probably thank him.

There was a clanging as the man pried the bar against the knob. A sharp, metallic clunk followed by a crunching sound, and the handle broke off. Jacob felt the fear build and backed up as he observed the handle drop on his side of the door. The man then jabbed at the knob and knocked away the core, creating a small peek hole where the knob had been.

I cannot allow him to enter, Jacob thought.

Jacob hung back in the shadows and looked at the small hole. He could see the whites of the man's eye as he peered in. The curtains were drawn and the room was pitch-black; Jacob knew the man couldn't see anything. Now was the time—if he was going to do it, he'd do it now. Jacob raised the pistol and aimed at the hole in the door. He'd shoot him through the eye. The gunshot would be loud, but a single shot would be hard for the things to pinpoint.

"Who's in there?" the man said.

Jacob eased back the pistol and held his breath.

"Come on now, I know someone's in there; I see your stuff on the bed."

Jacob held the pistol with both hands and sighted on the hole. He let his thumb quietly click off the safety then cock the hammer on the pistol, holding his breath.

"Whoa, okay now, I heard that; let's take it easy in there," the man said.

"Take it easy like you did on the boy and the girl?" Jacob asked, breaking the silence, trying to make his voice sound raucous.

"Come on now, I'm the only thing keeping them alive. The boy's got some growing up to do; I'm just trying to toughen him up."

"Yup, that's your business and you can keep it out there," Jacob said. "What do you want?"

"What do you got?"

Jacob forced a laugh, wanting the man to think he wasn't afraid, even if he was. He relaxed his shoulders and kept the gun aimed at the door. He could no longer see the man's eye but from the deflection of his voice, Jacob knew he was still resting in front of the door.

"You can have anything out there. I don't have enough in here to share. Take what you need, stay the night, but in the morning you need to be gone."

"Oh, come on now, you ain't left us shit out here. We gonna need something more. What you got? Food? Some water maybe?"

"What I got is a big-ass shotgun aimed at your head," Jacob bluffed. "I already made you my best offer. Take it or leave it."

Frank let out an exaggerated sigh. "Mister, I think we got off on the wrong foot here. We're all on the same side. I just need a little to keep us going. Hell, give us some of what you got, and maybe you can come with us. Lord knows I could use someone like you; that kid sure as hell ain't no help."

Jacob had no intention of letting the man in, but he wanted information from him. This was the first contact he'd had with anyone from the outside in days.

"Where are you going?" Jacob asked, intentionally leading the man on.

"The park; word is it's safe there. The military is running an evacuation," Frank said, relaxing his voice. Jacob heard the sound of a lighter as he lit another cigarette.

"Where did you hear this?" Jacob asked.

"State cop, two days ago," Frank answered.

"Bullshit, I haven't seen a cop since this all started."

"There's still some out there, mister. They stick to the highway, mostly. Won't go into the neighborhoods anymore."

"Then how is it you saw one?" Jacob asked suspiciously.

Frank grunted. "Stupid story, really. I actually made it the hell out of here… well, almost. My sister talked me into going back for her dumbass kid. The troopers had school buses up at the old high school, evacuating people. I got my family there, my sister and her little ones, but the woman refused to get on the bus. She begged me to go back for that one downstairs.

"I guess I am as stupid as he is for letting her talk me into it. Kid was holding up at the house with his girlfriend. I got 'em out of there, but shit was too far gone by the time we got back on the road. The siren that was going suddenly shutting off really screwed us. Seems like they're more active now than ever and running in those large groups."

"Have you… have you killed one?" Jacob asked.

A long pause. Jacob could hear Frank inhale deeply on the cigarette and let out a muffled cough. "Yeah, I've killed some. You?"

"Yeah," Jacob answered.

"Did you know them?"

"I knew the last ones; they were kids from up the street, but… but they were different," Jacob muttered.

"They weren't the people you thought they were. I'm not sure what's happening, but they aren't the same. This is no riot, brother; it's not civil unrest or revolution like the radio said. Shit ain't right out there—something's wrong, really wrong. I killed an old lady. She lived up the street from us, used a walker, and rarely left her front yard. That old bitch ran at me like a kid in her twenties. It's not right; that's not possible. I heard folks saying they from outer space, like an invasion!"

Jacob thought back to the blood on his hands, how it curled against the concrete floor. "That's nuts; I mean, Aliens? Really? No, it's not possible, right?" Jacob answered.

"Really? It ain't so crazy if you really stop to think about it."

"You said you knew the old lady, so how could she be from outer space?" Jacob asked unable to hide the sarcasm from his voice.

"Well... maybe not aliens, but shape shifters, something... That old woman, she wasn't an old women anymore, she even smelt differ—"

A large crash at the front of the house caused Jacob to jump. He gripped the pistol again and brought it up. "What was that?" Jacob asked.

Another large crash was followed by the scream from the girl downstairs—they were at the house.

"Come on, mister, you got to open this damn door!"

"What did you do? You brought them here!" Jacob shouted.

Sounds of shattering glass erupted from downstairs.

"I have to help them; when I get back you need to let us in!" Frank yelled.

Jacob heard Frank running down the stairs yelling, "I'm coming, Joey; hold on, boy!"

The yelling continued, Frank's voice no enraged shouting to the others. Jacob turned to his wife sitting behind him. "Get Katy to the attic."

"Come with us," Laura pleaded.

"I'll be right behind you."

Jacob moved closer to the door to listen. He heard the screams outside and more glass breaking below, followed by a shotgun blast. He ran to the closet where Laura was struggling to get the barely conscious Katy up the shelving. Jacob took his daughter from Laura and helped his wife up the shelf, using his shoulders to try to boost her up. He climbed as high as he could, then passed Katy to Laura through the hole in the ceiling and scrambled up after them. The house was shaking violently as he pulled himself up through the ceiling joists. He quickly moved to the center of the attic and kept his wife and daughter behind him as he looked over the access hole.

"We have to help them," Laura said, her voice trembling.

"There is nothing we can do for them," Jacob whispered.

Jacob shook his head and grabbed his wife and daughter in a tight hug as he listened to the screams below. Gunfire from the first floor, barely audible above the roar of the things bursting into his home, found its way through the rooms. The walls shook as it felt like hundreds of them must be pouring through his house. Jacob watched nervously while the ceiling joists swayed and rattled under the load of the things below. He left his wife's side and crawled across on his belly to the gable vent, wanting to see how many there were. He pressed his eye against the opening and peered into the street.

The front yard and street were filled with them. Shoulder to shoulder, they crowded and pushed their way into his home. The house heaved and shook with protest in rhythm to the movement of the mass. Jacob watched in fascination as the screaming suddenly stopped. The creatures halted their forward momentum and slowly withdrew. As quickly as they had massed, they collectively dispersed back into the shadows. The remaining ones in his home slowly bled back into the street. Jacob saw a tall man cradling the young girl's body, then another carrying the boy. Several others vacated the home before he witnessed the gruff man called Frank being dragged away.

"Where are they taking them?" Jacob whispered.

***

Thunder filled the night air as bold lightning strikes flashed in the distance. The flashes filled the bedroom with light through the gaps in the drapes, a strobe of patterns that played tricks on his mind as he watched the door. Laura was curled into the fetal position beside him, cradling Katy as they slept in the center of the bed. Jacob held the rifle in his hand, splitting his time watching the bedroom door and peeking through the window. He tried to sleep, but every slap of thunder thrust him awake so hard it made his chest hurt.

Two hours had passed since the things left the house without even trying the second floor, never even moving to the steps. They kept all of their focus on the visitors below, and the pack left with them in their clutches. Jacob had watched them move away and vanish from the street, leaving things as if they'd never been there. He'd then waited until he was sure the things were gone before returning his family to the bedroom.

Jacob lay on the bed, listening to the sound of raindrops beating on the roof, the cadence slowly increasing as the storm intensified and moved over them. He let his feet touch the floor and moved to the window. Pulling back the drapes, he saw that the street was filling with water. Without power, the pumps would be down and basements would soon backup. The cars were still there; the dead man's body hanging out and soaked in the pouring rain. He looked across the street at the ruins of Smitty's home.

Jacob thought of Frank's story of the evacuation at the school. How he had to go back for his nephew himself. There was no rescue; they had to do it on their own. "Nobody's coming," he whispered. "Nobody."

A stirring in the bed snapped his gaze from the street. He turned and watched as Laura propped herself up on one arm and looked at him. "Anything?" she asked.

Jacob shook his head and closed the drape before walking back to the bed. He sat down lightly at the edge, close enough that Laura could put an arm on his shoulder. A loud rolling of thunder rattled the house, and Jacob flinched with the noise. "Come to bed; lie down with us," Laura whispered. "There's nothing you can do."

Chapter 5

There was a distant, low rumbling noise and muffled voices when Jacob opened his eyes. He imagined it was a dream until he heard them again, along with the growl of a diesel engine. He jumped from the bed and hurried to the window. Down the street, he saw a small military convoy moving slowly and deliberately. Green painted trucks, with men walking along beside them, headed in Jacob's direction. The convoy stopped just in front of his wrecked car.

A Humvee, with a man standing in the turret over a large machine gun, led two large transport vehicles. As soon as they stopped, more soldiers dismounted the vehicles and stood near the curbs with their rifles out. Ignoring the destroyed homes, another group of soldiers ran to the remaining intact front doors, pounding on them and calling out for survivors.

Jacob watched in amazement as homes that he'd presumed were abandoned opened their doors. People were guided out and hurried to line up at the backs of the trucks. Soldiers tossed in bags and helped men, women, and children climb steps to board the vehicles.

Rescue! They're here! Jacob thought.

"Now! We have to go now!" Jacob yelled, jumping to his feet and waking his wife.

Grabbing the cordless drill, he removed the screws from the door as quickly as he could.

He grabbed the rifle, slung it across his back, and placed the pistol in its holster. His wife was fumbling with the backpack. Jacob grabbed it from her and put it over her shoulder, then lifted Katy. He grabbed Laura by the wrist and pulled her behind him as he ran for the stairs. He rushed for the already open front door, weaving through the overturned furniture and stepping over the remains of the splintered front door. Jacob worried when he saw that the trucks were nearly filled. He called out and caught the attention of a soldier who was near his porch.

"Show me your eyes!" the soldier ordered, aiming the rifle.

Jacob stopped and raised his hands staring at the soldier. "We're okay, we are all fine."

The soldier looked them over and pointed a gloved finger at Katy lying in Jacob's arms. "What's with the little one?"

"She is just sick; she needs a doctor."

The soldier stepped in and looked at Jacob closely then down at Katy. He frowned sympathetically and nodded his head. "Okay. Quickly, we gotta keep moving." The soldier then yelled over his shoulder, "We got three more over here."

Jacob rushed his wife and daughter ahead of him to the back of the first transport. A soldier was just beginning to close the canopy. "Sorry, sir, this one is full; try the other truck." Jacob looked at the man in shock. He knew there would be no arguing with him so he grabbed his wife's arm and dragged her to the second transport.

The soldier had already removed the stepladder and closed the gate, but when he looked at Jacob and Katy, his mouth dropped upon seeing the sick girl. "It's okay. We can make room. Lift her up!" he said, locking eyes with Jacob.

Jacob lifted his daughter at the back gate. Someone grabbed her and pulled her on board the truck. He could hear Katy's screams as he lost sight of her. He hugged his wife and went to lift her over the tailgate. From above, a man in a flannel shirt put his hand in her face and pushed her away. "Truck is full, man!" he yelled.

A second soldier stepped forward, put a hand on Jacob's shoulder, and said, "It's okay; you two can walk with us."

"My daughter is alone in there," Jacob yelled. "Just let my wife on."

He turned and looked at Laura. "Don't worry, I'll find you," he said before he lifted her again.

The soldier helped lift Laura, and as she grabbed the top of the truck's tailgate, a woman on board grabbed her hand and tried to help pull her in. The man in flannel again came forward; he tried to peel Laura's fingers from the gate then went to push an open palm to her face. "I said the truck is—"

Not allowing him to finish, Jacob let go of his wife and grabbed the man's wrist. He lifted his leg to the tailgate and pulled back.

The flannelled man lost his balance and tumbled head first from the bed of the truck and out to the street. Hitting hard against the pavement, he lay motionless. Jacob watched as his wife was lifted up and over the tailgate. A soldier moved Jacob aside and began fastening down the canopy as shots erupted from behind them. Jacob spun to see a black-eyed man sprinting toward them, but—already—soldiers were online, firing. Jacob watched as the thing dropped and rolled to the ground as more fast-moving runners came into view from down the street.

"Go, go, go," a soldier yelled, slapping the side of the truck. "Let's go, friend, keep up," the soldier said, turning Jacob around and pushing him forward.

Jacob stared as the truck slowly moved away. With the gunfire erupting all around him and not knowing what else to do, he chased after it. He watched as the soldiers fell in beside him, turning often to check their rear for pursuers. They were moving fast but not fast enough; the truck was pulling away and the mob was closing on them.

Jacob heard screams of agony as the swarm overcame the man in flannel. The soldiers stopped; one of them grabbed Jacob and turned him toward the center of a quickly forming protective ring. Jacob looked at his surroundings and realized he was the last civilian remaining on the street, encased in the human shield provided by this group of soldiers. Hearing the screams and seeing the black eyes approach, Jacob swung the rifle from his back and held it tightly in his arms.

"Make 'em count, boys!" a soldier yelled.

The soldiers fired with chaotic precision. Jacob watched them take quick shots into the crowd and work as a team, covering each other as another reloaded. Jacob moved to an edge and prepared to fire but was quickly pushed back to the center. Once the initial wave was cut down, the men were back on their feet, shouting orders, and directing Jacob in the direction the trucks had gone. The mob began to close in again; Jacob saw the Humvee as it circled back over the sidewalk and lawns. Its engine at a high roar, it raced past them and skidded to a stop in the street. With the Humvee shielding them from the advancing swarm, the big gun on its roof let loose a barrage. A thump, thump, thump resonated from the big gun up in the turret, ripping the charging mass apart.

Following the soldiers, Jacob ran and took cover behind the Humvee with two other men. The big gun cut down wave after wave of the charging forms while other soldiers covered the sides and backs. The gunfire became deafening; it disoriented Jacob, and he put his hands to his ringing ears. When the gunner stopped firing, the street was suddenly quiet. Jacob turned and saw through the billowing blue smoke that the transports had moved on in the chaos.

The tight mass of soldiers began reloading magazines while holding their position and watching the surrounding neighborhood. Jacob felt lost in the group, and he looked to the soldier next to him. The man was middle aged—maybe late thirties—and looked like he hadn't slept for days. His weather-beaten face was dirty and stubbly with the makings of an early beard. He wore a tattered army uniform; the sleeves were torn, and there was a long rip in one pant leg of his trousers. The man's knees and elbows were covered in dirt and blood.

"Where did they go?" Jacob asked.

Pushing loose bullets into a magazine, the soldier replied, "Back to the park. We're staging folks there before moving everyone north." The soldier finished with his task and looked up at Jacob. Seeming to notice the way Jacob looked him over, he continued, "Yeah, I ain't much to look at; it's been a rough week."

"Sorry, I didn't mean to stare."

The solder waved his hand, dismissing Jacob's apology. "You know, I saw what you did back there," the soldier said. "The man on the truck."

"I won't apologize. He wouldn't let my wife on the truck," Jacob said.

"Yeah… he was an asshole. I've lost a lot of good men the last few days. I won't be shedding any tears for that one," the soldier replied and then extending a gloved hand. "By the way, my name's Murphy."

Jacob returned the handshake. "I'm Jacob."

Murphy gripped Jacob's hand firmly and pulled him in close so the others couldn't hear. "Listen, I ain't gonna sugarcoat this for you. They'll be back and when they come, they'll come hard. You need to get that weapon up and be ready to use it; do you understand? You can't cower."

"I got it," Jacob said, suddenly unsure of himself and missing the security of his second-floor safe zone.

More screams erupted from all around them, signifying the things were out there roaming the backyards of the homes.

"Well, that didn't take long," Murphy said under his breath. The soldier then rose to his feet and yelled as he brought up the rifle, "Lock and load, boys—it's time to pay the bills!"

The mob had somehow managed to completely surround their position. Instead of coming back at them from down the street, they had slipped through the backyards and were pouring at them from between the houses. The turret gun opened up, sweeping and hitting everything it could, and the soldiers on both sides of Jacob fired their rifles. Jacob pulled the .22 rifle tight to his shoulder and took aim before pulling the trigger, switching targets until his only magazine was empty. Then he drew the handgun from its holster.

The deranged things had gotten in close. He watched as a soldier was hit from behind and knocked to the street. A black-eyed man tried to drag him away, and as another soldier went to his aid, he was quickly taken down with him. More climbed over the hood of the Humvee and swamped the mounted machine gunner from behind. The gun fired wildly, the gunner refusing to be taken down without a fight.

Jacob looked up the street in the direction the trucks had moved. He stood and contemplated running after them. His hands were shaking with fear. His ears were ringing from the close proximity of the gunshots, the screams blocking out his thoughts. He raised his pistol when he saw another wave of the mob closing on him. He aimed straight into the chest of the closest one and fired until the slide locked to the rear.

They were all over him now; they leapt and tackled him to the ground, then more piled on. Jacob tried to fight back but was pressed against the pavement with his head turned to the side. He could feel the things tugging at his legs, trying to drag him off. He heard the clang on the street beside him and recognized the round metallic object that was rolling in his direction. He closed his eyes tight and waited for the explosion he was sure would come.

Chapter 6

The ceiling was made up of evenly spaced old wooden beams; holes had been drilled through them and strands of wire were stretched between each timber. Heavy wooden floorboards with small breaks between them allowed bright light to filter in. The rays cut his pupils, causing them to contract; he closed his eyes. He heard heavy footsteps above him and clomping of heavy feet. Scattered dust drifted through the beams of light and he watched pieces of earth slowly fall until they touched his face. He lay staring at the ceiling as if in a dream; his eyes open and aware, he stayed immobile waiting for his body to catch up with his brain.

Suddenly, Jacob jerked and stiffened as the feelings of pain and fear filled his body. He tried to sit up—until agony shot through his shoulder and hip. Jacob looked down and saw that a green field dressing covered his wounded side. He felt the pressure of a heavy hand on his chest.

"Whoa there, big guy; just relax," a soothing voice whispered.

"Wha… where am I? Where's my family? Where are Laura and Katy?" Jacob asked, breathing heavily. Still struggling to sit up, he knew he needed to relax but couldn't fight off the fear. His heart was

73

beating out of his chest and he felt the sweat gather on his forehead.

The soldier scooted closer and Jacob recognized the face of Murphy, the soldier he had met on the street. "I need you to stay quiet; okay, buddy?" Murphy whispered as he pointed to the ceiling. "Can you do that for me?"

Confused and angry at being spoken to like a child, Jacob glared at the man. He wanted to get to his feet, to escape, to find the trucks. He needed to get to Laura and Katy.

Jacob was about to protest again when he heard more hollow, heavy steps on the plank floor above. They slowly faded and were followed by a loud slap of a screen door. Against a far wall, Jacob saw a tall black soldier standing on an old crate and looking out a narrow window. The man turned and looked back in his direction.

"They gone, Sergeant; all of 'em. Just moved back down Oak Street."

"Shit. That's the third time they've been through this house, not sure how long our luck is going to hold," Murphy whispered.

Jacob moved his good arm behind him, pushed, and forced himself into a sitting position. Feeling bolts of pain fire through his trembling body, he scooted so that his back rested against a rough block wall.

"You said Oak Street? Where the hell am I? What happened back there?" Jacob asked.

Murphy looked down at him with concern. "You need to relax. Just chill for a bit and let those wounds set up. You took some frag from that grenade."

The other soldier walked away from the window and sat against the wall near Jacob. "It was superficial, but damn, you're a bleeder. I patched you up and ended up using all the damn med kit on your ass," the soldier said.

Jacob looked down, letting his hand tenderly touch the bandage. "Thank you… I guess. Wait, where… where's my family?" Jacob stuttered.

"They're safe; I'm sure they made it back—" Murphy started to say before Jacob interrupted him.

"Then you don't know!" Jacob said his voice rising.

Murphy raised a finger to his lips and pointed at the floor above. "I said you need to be quiet."

Stephens shook his head, watching Jacob complain. "Fools, man… we never shoulda stopped for that last set. We'd be back on the base behind the walls if we'd just kept going. Hell… I should have never reported to duty at all. I should have stayed home." The soldier swung his head down to hold it in his hands. "I'd be downstate right now, quiet and comfy."

"Cut it, Corporal; our job is to collect civilians, not take care of our own asses," Murphy said.

"Man, that's bullshit. Who gonna care for all them civilians now, with Second Squad gone?" Stephens muttered as he looked down and dug through a small pack. He reached in and pulled a small bottle of water and handed it to Jacob. "Here, drink this down. You lost a lot of blood, need to replace those fluids." Stephens reached back into his bag and removed Jacob's pistol. "Take this too. I topped off the mag for you. I seen you in action back there. Next time, slow down and aim; you'd have better luck with it."

Jacob held the pistol in his hand. Ignoring the water, he said, "I don't understand how I got here? Who are you?"

"Hmmh," Stephens grunted. "Some appreciation that is… Guess you took a hard thump to the grape. Yeah, I'd be jacked up in the head too."

"Dammit, just tell me what in the hell is going on. Where's my family?" Jacob shouted, trying again to get to his feet.

Murphy put his hand up, silencing Jacob. "I already told you, your family is safe. I think so anyway; the base is locked up tight and those things haven't gotten in yet. Now… like I said before, you need to chill. If those wounds get to bleeding again, we'll be stuck here."

Jacob exhaled loudly, his frustration growing. "Where is here?"

Jacob watched Murphy reach into his pack and pull out a brown plastic pouch the size of a large book. He used his knife to open the package, and then dumped smaller packages on the floor in front of him. "We're in the basement of a house on Oak. You should be more grateful, seeing as how we carried your ass… well, Stephens did mostly—"

"You're welcome," Stephens sounded off. "You heavy as hell too, ya know… wouldn't kill you to do some PT, lose some of that gut."

Jacob looked down and removed the cap from the bottle he was holding. "Oak Street? That's only three blocks over from my house."

"Like I said, you heavy," Stephens answered, glaring.

Murphy pointed at the window. "We barely made it in here, as it is. We were able to cut down the last wave. The grenade helped, but we had to move before they rebounded—they always fucking rebound. You're damn lucky we decided to take you with us."

"I'd ha' left ya if it was up to me," Stephens said, shaking his head. "Hell, Sergeant here, guess he figures better to take you with us than fight you later."

Jacob stared at him blankly. "What's that supposed to mean?"

"It means every time we lose someone, they come back as the fucking darkness."

"The darkness?" Jacob asked.

"Those, things, whatever the hell they are," Stephens said, moving away to a far wall and dropping down against it. He pulled his rifle into his lap and cradled it.

"What is it? The Darkness… is it like a sickness?"

"Hell no; it's an actual thing, like a whole new person," Stephens muttered, shaking his head.

Jacob, again, found himself losing his patience. "You're talking nonsense!"

Murphy looked up from the bag in his lap and pointed at him. "I won't warn you again to keep your voice down. I can tape that mouth shut, if you'd prefer it." Murphy dug into the plastic pouches in front of him and tossed Jacob a sealed package. "Eat this; you need the calories."

Murphy put his knife back into a sheath on his belt. "It's not a sickness; it's… it's something different."

Jacob took the package, flipped it over, read the "pound cake" label, and set it on the floor next to him. "Sorry. I'm not in the mood for cake."

"Then go ahead and eat it, because that shit is in no way cake. If you're going to be strong enough to travel with us, you need to eat," Murphy ordered.

Jacob took the foil package and ripped off the top. He looked at the yellow brick inside, and then looked back at Murphy. "I've seen them close up.

The black eyes, the dark mouths, and their blood… it… it was like oil," he said quietly.

Stephens grunted. "That's cause they ain't people; they the darkness. We already told you that."

"What does that mean?" Jacob asked, frustrated and looking at Murphy as he pulled the yellow brick from the wrapper.

"The Darkness, Zulus, Marble Eyes, Boogie Man—whatever you call them, it's all the same," Murphy said, spooning through his meal. "They are not us, not anymore."

Murphy opened a drinking tube hanging from his vest and sucked water into his mouth, taking a long swallow. He stared at Jacob, then looked at Stephens who was leaning against the wall. "You been cut off since the beginning of this, huh?"

Jacob nodded. "We haven't left the house since the sirens turned on. I saw the early news reports about the rioting and the PSA to shelter in place," Jacob said, breaking off a hunk of the brick and putting it in his mouth. He made an odd face and took a long swig of water to wash down the substance.

Stephens pulled his rifle away from his lap. "Damn PSA; shoulda told people to run, get as far away as you can. Now we got so many pockets of people trapped in the city and they just waiting to get taken… soon they's all be gone, be one of them."

"So what are they?" Jacob asked.

Stephens spit on the floor near his boot. "I don't know what they are," he said, his voice rising. Catching himself, he turned back to Jacob and spoke in a low voice. "Doc Jersey, our medic, he cut one open after we killed it. No guts, man, just a black jelly glob all up in their bodies. We tried taking one prisoner… yeah, we captured and hog-tied its ass. They strong, but they ain't no supermen. This thing was weird, though; the damn thing screamed until it died. We didn't do a damn thing to it. It just fucking died, man. Then it dried up like a choked-out fish."

"It's true; they shrivel up… like dehydrate," Murphy said.

Jacob's jaw dropped, not understanding but seeing a connection. "The ones I killed; the blood, it shriveled and dried up too, like old paint—"

There was a loud thump on the floor above as a door slammed open. Stephens held a hand up and put a finger to his lip. Jacob looked up at the ceiling and watched the shadows as a figure walked over the planks. It paced through the house and then quickly left again.

Stephens quietly got to his feet and stepped lightly to the window. He looked out to search the street, then moved back to his position and looked down at Murphy. "Sergeant, we can't stay here. That's the fourth time they checked this place. They know we're close."

Chapter 7

Jacob stood pressed against the wall with Murphy to his front. He was blinded in the night and kept a hand on Murphy's shoulder so he could be guided by him. Stephens had already cleared the basement doorway and advanced out into the shadows to scout the way ahead. They were waiting for his signal to proceed outside. A low clicking sound came to Jacob's ears and Murphy turned, looked at Jacob, and waved him forward. The soldier then stepped off, pulling Jacob behind him. Once in the doorway, they pressed back against the wall. Jacob looked around, trying to orient himself before stepping up the concrete steps to the outside. He was shocked to make it up them without falling on his face.

Murphy moved quickly along the side of the house, then knelt beside a tall bush. He looked back at Jacob and lifted his night vision goggles from his eyes. "You all right?" he whispered.

"I can't see anything," Jacob whispered back.

"Just keep a hand on my back until your eyes adjust… You good?"

Jacob nodded even though the pain in his hip seemed unbearable and was causing bolts of burning spikes to shoot to his spine. Not wanting to stop, he clenched his teeth and whispered back, "I'm good."

"Okay then, Stephens is just ahead. I know you can't see him in the dark, but it'll get better as we go. Just stay close and keep your mouth shut, walk when I walk, stop when I stop, and if I run… try to keep up."

Murphy stepped off briskly, hugging the front face of the house and moving south in the direction that Jacob knew would take them to the park. They stayed away from the sidewalk, crouching beside shrubs, moving between cars parked in driveways, and sometimes jumping a fence. When they came to a cross street, Stephens would duck near the corner of a house to wait for Murphy and Jacob to bunch up behind. Murphy would slap the tall man's shoulder and he would dart across the street, the sound of his boots slapping the pavement and filling the dead air.

A signal invisible to Jacob's naked eyes was received, and Murphy got back to his feet, dragging Jacob behind him. As promised, his night vision slowly improved as they traveled. He was able to make out the shapes of houses, then objects in the yards. Now he could see nearly everything up to a short distance, and Jacob slowly recognized the neighborhood they were in. He often used this route as a shortcut when going to Katy's daycare.

The streets were lined with well-manicured lawns on both sides. Many of the homes here looked untouched; the doors remained closed and windows were in place. Jacob found that more and more of the driveways were absent of vehicles as he traveled the neighborhood. Were they evacuated? Jacob pondered as he passed another long, empty driveway. They rounded the corner of a tall brick-faced house and suddenly, a bright floodlight filled a front yard. For a moment, Jacob could see the crouched figure of Stephens freeze just before he sprinted out of sight and vanished.

Jacob was turned back by Murphy before being rushed to the side of the house. They knelt down next to the side of the home in a dark shadow and away from the light. Murphy flipped up his goggles and raised his rifle to search the area lit by the floodlight. He scanned left and right as the area, again, suddenly went dark. Murphy pulled the rifle back into his chest and dropped his goggles. He crouched lower and pressed his body against the wall.

Jacob couldn't contain himself and whispered, "What's going on?"

"Nothing; probably just one of those damn solar security lights, tied to a motion sensor," Murphy answered. "Come on follow—"

A loud sound of feet falling on the sidewalk silenced Murphy. They both pressed tight against the brick house as several figures passed by within yards of their position. The Others moved beyond them, and the floodlight kicked on again, lighting the neighboring yard but this time, also illuminating six figures. They stood together but randomly spread across the yard—not searching, just standing in the center of the brightly lit space.

Murphy pushed Jacob back around the corner then skirted ahead of him to lead the way to the brick home's backyard. They moved up a narrow walkway that brought them to a tight stone path between the house and a detached garage. Murphy moved through it with Jacob close behind. They rounded a stack of overflowing metal trashcans, then dropped low in the grass and continued on to the far side of the yard where they met up with a tall picket fence.

Murphy low-walked the distance to the fence and knelt down with his back to the wooden slats. They were now directly behind the brick house and all the way to the back of the lot. Next door, was the home with the solar light in the front yard. Behind them, over the fence, was a narrow patch of high grass and trees that divided the lot from the home on the opposite side of the block.

Murphy had his goggles down and was looking ahead at the brick house. He then lifted his rifle and probed the area of the neighboring backyard. "Three more of the damn lights up there by the roof," he whispered.

Three quick shots, followed by two more, blasted from the front of the neighboring home. Murphy leapt to his feet, turned, and pulled Jacob up beside him. "Time to keep up," he said and took off running toward the neighboring fence. When he got there, he let his rifle hang from a sling and cupped his hands, providing a step for Jacob.

"What are you doing?" Jacob asked.

"I'll give you a boost. Get over and don't stop until you hit the next yard."

"But the lights—" He was interrupted by a long scream and volley of gunfire, this time farther away.

Murphy flexed his arms. "Let's go; you're wasting time!"

Jacob shook his head and lifted a foot into the soldier's grip. He stood up and grabbed the top edge of the fence as he felt Murphy pushing him up and over. He cleared the top lip of the fence and fell hard to the grass on the far side. He scrambled back to his feet; the pain in his hip sent electrical shocks up his left side. Jacob had just stepped off in the darkness with his hands in front of him when the backyard exploded with bright light.

Three bright halogen lights, attached to the roof's gables, kicked on simultaneously. Jacob looked directly into one, filling his vision with spots and momentarily blinding him. He heard Murphy thump to the ground beside him and felt a hand shove him forward.

"What are you still doing here?" Murphy yelled. "Run!"

Murphy again shoved him forward, causing him to almost trip. He ran past Jacob with his rifle up, sweeping the yard as he bolted to the opposite end. He nearly crashed into the fence when he stopped and aimed toward the front yard to wait for Jacob to catch up. Murphy, again, dropped the rifle to the sling and dropped his cupped hands. Without argument, Jacob lifted a foot to the gloved hands and felt himself being lifted up and over the fence. Again, he dropped fast to the other side and landed hard as he impacted with the ground.

Gracefully, Murphy dropped down beside him and pulled Jacob to his feet by the back of his shirt. Once more, they were up and running through backyards—fortunately ones without fences. Murphy slowed to a jog, then to a brisk walk. He kept his rifle up as he continued forward and scanned ahead. At the corner lot, Murphy stopped and moved in closer to the back of a home. He paused just off a back patio that led up to a room filled with furniture.

Murphy held up a hand, halting Jacob, then pointed a finger at the patio door. Walking low with his back to the wall, he approached the patio. As Jacob watched, Murphy lightly walked up the steps to a large deck before he crept to a sliding patio door. Moments later, the door slid open and Murphy waved Jacob forward as he disappeared inside. Jacob took a deep breath and followed the soldier into the home.

The patio door opened into a dining room dimly lit by the floodlights from down the street. The space smelled of death and rotting food. A round wooden table held a carton of milk that was knocked over; its spoiled contents splashed across the table and onto the floor. Jacob closed the door and followed Murphy deeper into the house. In the living room, they found piled luggage and an open closet with coats and shoes spilling out.

"They left in a hurry," Murphy whispered as he walked to a partial wall banking an open staircase. He pulled back a curtain to allow more of the light to pour in and peered into the front yard.

"Is Stephens out there?" Jacob asked.

"Somewhere… he's smart; he'll find a tidy spot where he can watch for us."

"Why did he fire, you sure they didn't get him?"

Murphy clenched his jaw, looking to the front yard. "They might have gotten the jump on him, but more likely he was providing a diversion for us—"

A noise near the front of the house caused Jacob to drop down and pull his elbows in. Murphy heard it too and dropped the curtain. In one fluid motion, he spun on his heels, pressed his back to the wall, and brought up his rifle. Murphy looked across the room at Jacob and pointed to the kitchen. Jacob nodded then turned and moved quietly across the floor to get behind a kitchen island. He knelt down, his head just out of sight.

An already partially open door squeaked as it swung inward, bleeding more light into the room and backlighting the cabinets over Jacob's head. More noise echoed through the space with the sound of a vase or pot being tipped over and rolling loudly across a hardwood floor. Jacob squatted lower as he heard wet shoes squeaking on the waxed wood floors. They moved closer and seemed to stop just beyond the kitchen. After a short pause, they moved again and stopped at the island. Jacob could hear the thing's breath and the rustle of its clothing as it moved its hand over items on the island. A glass was knocked over; it rolled across the island's surface and dropped to the floor, shattering at Jacob's feet.

A shard of glass slid and rested against Jacob's boot; it rattled and chimed with the shaking of his knee. He held his breath and tried to stop his trembling. Finding it impossible, he steeled his nerve, gripped the pistol, and rose to face whatever was there. He stumbled as he stood too quickly and caused blood to rush from his head. His already weak knees taking him off- balance, Jacob dropped a hand to the island to steady himself as he looked into the blackened eyes of a broad-shouldered man. He was wearing a collared work shirt with one sleeve ripped free, a pink and black tie still knotted around his neck.

The thing looked through Jacob like it was focusing on the wall behind him. Its lips curled back to reveal glistening ivory fangs and blackened gums. Suddenly, the thing's arms shot out. Reaching for Jacob, it lunged forward over the island. It opened its mouth to yell but was halted by Murphy leaping from out of the dark and landing on the thing's back. Murphy quickly wrapped his forearm around its mouth to block the scream from escaping. Pulling a knife with his free hand, he shoved the blade into the creature's neck. Together they flew over the island and crashed into Jacob, the three of them dropping hard to the tile floor.

Murphy held on until the thing stopped moving then rose above it, continuing to stab at the base of its neck. When the black-eyed man finally stopped twitching, he pulled his arm away and rested back on his ankles. Jacob struggled below them and pulled himself clear. Murphy dropped back to his rear and scooted until he was across the kitchen, pressed against the refrigerator. Jacob continued to crawl away toward the light then rolled to his back and looked up at the ceiling.

Breathing hard, he pushed himself to a sitting position and nursed his wounded hip. The thing's head was turned in his direction; its blank eyes seemed to glare at him as the black, oily blood drained from its neck onto the tile floor. Jacob looked across the kitchen at Murphy, who reached up and ripped a decorative towel from the refrigerator handle then used it to wipe the blade of his knife.

Murphy rolled to his knees and climbed to his feet. He pulled open the refrigerator door then looked away as a stench hit him. He looked back and, cupping a hand over the end of his flashlight, looked through the fridge again. Pulling out a bottle of water, he closed the door and twisted the cap from the bottle. He drank half of it and, on his return to the living room, tossed the rest to Jacob as he walked past him.

"Get up; we've got to move," Murphy whispered.

Chapter 8

The solar light went out and stayed out. The house and yard were dark—no sign of the things. Murphy moved them to the front of the house where they hid on a large, open front porch. A wood swing hanging from the rafters squeaked as the wind moved it.

"There," Murphy whispered, pointing in the distance.

Murphy held out his goggles and put them to Jacob's eye. Jacob blinked and let his vision adjust to the optics. Up ahead, on the opposite corner, a light flashed. Jacob dropped the goggles. Looking in the same direction, he now saw nothing.

"You can't see it without the NODs; it's infrared. I have one just like it," Murphy whispered while removing a small chip holding a tiny bulb. Murphy manipulated the device connecting the battery then held it over his head. "He's in the scrub brush. How well do you know that area?"

Jacob looked back at him confused. "I… I don't know it at all. I mean, it's just a few empty lots… was supposed to be developed—"

"Buddy, I don't need a real estate lecture. Do you know what's on the other side of it?"

Jacob looked back to the distant tree line. "It moves out from here. There is a railroad bed at the back of the lots; that's the reason they never sold… I mean, there's railroad tracks back there, then past that and through the trees is a two-lane highway."

"Route 30?" Murphy asked.

Jacob nodded and watched as Murphy pulled a small spiral notebook from a pocket on his sleeve. He began to sketch their location, then scribbled notes that Jacob couldn't make out. Murphy folded over the page and stuck the notebook back in his pocket. "Okay, that should bring us out on the approach to the safe zone. You ready to move?"

"What about the motion light?" Jacob asked.

"Well, either those things are gone, or the battery died. You can't go home, and we can't stay here."

"I understand."

"Good; I'll run with you to the corner and stop. You keep going and head to the trees. Slow down to a walk when you cross the street; Stephens will find you."

Jacob nodded as a response. Murphy slapped him on the shoulder and climbed to his feet. Slowly, the soldier led them off the porch with his rifle up. They moved quietly, walking a narrow path leading from the stoop to the main sidewalk. Jacob's eyes had adjusted to the moonlight, and he could see a good distance in all directions. Murphy picked up his pace, and Jacob followed, running along and staying just behind Murphy's right shoulder.

Just as he'd said he would do, Murphy stopped at the curb and quickly turned to cover the direction they'd traveled. Exactly as he was told to, Jacob ran past him. Continuing into the street and running for the wooded lots, his footfalls echoed off the pavement. Halfway across, gunshots erupted from behind him. He continued on his way and sprinted for the cover of the woods. When he hit the grass—instead of stopping as instructed—he kept going, the adrenaline pushing him on. Muzzle flashes from deep in the trees ahead blinded him as tracers cut just to the right of his path.

Jacob ran on, his foot catching in a hole and causing him to tumble forward. He dropped into a shallow embankment. He instinctively lowered his hands to try to cushion his fall, only to have them cut open on the sharp gravel. He ducked his head as he rolled, crashing through a thorn bush at the bottom. Gunfire continued as Jacob crawled forward deeper into the lot. Feeling cuts to his hands and face, he dragged his battered body away from the sounds. Suddenly, a hand from behind lifted him back to his feet and he heard Stephens' voice.

"Run!"

Wet branches slapped his face; thorns tore at his shirt and dug into his skin. He ducked and turned, running for the open ground he saw ahead and praying it would be the railroad bed that would provide cover. Bullets snapped around him; the sounds echoed off the canopy of the trees as the muzzle flashes confused his vision. Jacob took long staggering steps, struggling to put one foot in front of the other as his lungs burned and he gasped for air.

He hit the railroad bed and again fell to his hands and knees. Scrambling to the top of it, he ran across the first rail, tripped over the second, and rolled down the other side. He crawled forward; disoriented, gasping for air, bile in his stomach begging him to vomit. He fought the urge to collapse as his arms and legs cramped from fear and exhaustion. He crawled on until Murphy moved up beside him. He felt himself being pummeled and pressed to the ground as someone dropped on top of him, and a gloved hand cupped his mouth, forcing him to take whistling breaths through his nose.

"Shhhhh, quiet," Murphy whispered in his ear.

Jacob closed his eyes, trying to control his breathing. A crash of footfalls tumbled over the summit of the railroad bed; stones clanged against the tracks as they ran across and into the brush on both sides. Jacob's body flinched uncontrollably from fear and adrenalin. Murphy pinned him to ground tighter, and Jacob, putting trust in the soldier, resisted the urge to break free. He pressed his eyes closed, allowing his face to be pressed against the dirt and tasting the leather glove held tight over his mouth. The things ran to the left and right of him so close, he could feel the breeze off their legs racing by as bits of mud and grass were kicked onto his cheek.

They slowly faded away with the sounds of the breaking tree limbs, moving farther east. Murphy rolled off of him and popped up to a knee. Jacob saw that Stephens had joined them in a small depression at the base of the embankment. Murphy and Stephens held their rifles steady as they slowly scanned the area. Jacob lay silent, still catching his breath, trying to control his heartbeat, and pushing back the pain radiating through his body.

After what seemed an eternity, Murphy looked down at him and asked, "Are you okay?"

"Hell, no. I'm not okay," Jacob responded.

"Good." Murphy handed Jacob a plastic bottle. "Drink some water; we'll be moving shortly."

Jacob took the bottle and pushed himself up to his knees, then rocked back to a sitting position. The rifle was still over his shoulder and, somehow, he'd manage not to drop the pistol through all of it. He lifted the bottle to his lips and took a sip. Murphy looked at him, scowling.

"Finish it; you never know when you'll get another chance," he said.

Jacob tipped the bottle back, gulped the remainder of the water, and then let it rest in the weeds beside him. He put his hand to his hip and moved his fingers over the medical tape, feeling the curled edges and the dampness of the bandage. Jacob knew it had come loose in one of the falls he'd taken, but it could wait; he wanted to keep moving and make it to the park as soon as possible.

Without saying a word, Stephens got to his feet, then dropped a hand to pull Murphy up; in turn, Murphy reached a hand to Jacob. They stood silently. For the moment, the woods seemed safer than the neighborhood; the tall trees provided concealment for their movement. Stephens, again, led the way, slowly stepping through thick cover until he located a game trail. Jacob watched as he took careful steps, lifting his feet and cautiously putting them down to avoid branches and leaves.

They stopped often to listen, sometimes kneeling in the brush and vegetation waiting for a suspicious sound to fade. They could still hear the black-eyes moving, although they were far off. Jacob could hear the distant snapping brush and splashing of water as the things continued searching for them. Stephens pressed forward until the trio reached the two-lane highway, where he dropped to his belly and crawled to the mowed shoulder of the road.

The moon was high in the sky now; its bright face lit the blacktop surface of the road, making it easier to see. Murphy pushed Jacob ahead, and soon the three of them were shoulder to shoulder at the highway's edge. It was surprisingly empty and devoid of vehicles. Jacob expected abandoned cars and a deadlocked traffic jam; instead, he looked over a silent roadway. The buildings on the far side all appeared to be empty and surprisingly untouched. The road rose away from them and off to the right. At the top of the hill sat a police patrol car blocking the road.

Stephens had his rifle to his eye and was inspecting the vehicle. He pulled his eye away from the rifle's optics and whispered, "There's people in the car."

Jacob twisted while trying to get a better view of the vehicle that was a hundred yards away, but it was hard to pick out anything in the dark. Backlit by the horizon, the light bar on the top made it stand out from the grey-blue sky behind it. Jacob squinted; he could just barely make out movement from inside the vehicle. Murphy scooted back away from the shoulder, and then started to crawl in the direction of the car.

"What are you doing?" Stephens asked.

"Let's check it out. Stay close behind me."

Murphy continued crawling in the direction of the patrol car. Jacob felt a pat on his back and looked back at Stephens who motioned for him to follow.

"You heard the sergeant, we're gonna check it out," Stephens whispered.

Chapter 9

It was slow going crawling through the tall grass toward the patrol car. Jacob watched Murphy and tried to mimic his motions—every movement deliberate and quiet as they slipped through the blades of grass. Murphy held his rifle in his right hand by the sling, near the barrel. He would push his arm forward, then slowly allow the rest of his body to crawl ahead. He'd stay motionless, listening, and then lift his head to survey the area before moving his rifle arm again to repeat the movement.

One arm length at a time, they moved along the depression at the side of the road. Jacob didn't dare lift his head to look. He stayed as low to the ground as possible, trying to become one with it, and wishing he was thinner so that he could bury himself in the weeds. Every time he pushed himself ahead with his feet, he felt the wound on his hip grind against the soil.

Keeping the pain to himself, he didn't yelp or cringe. He didn't want to be a burden or give the soldiers an excuse to stop. Jacob desperately wanted to reach the evacuation site, and he knew he couldn't do it without the men escorting him. Jacob reached an arm out ahead and slapped into Murphy's calf. In his agony and trying to push his thoughts aside, he hadn't noticed that Murphy had stopped. Jacob pulled back his arm and waited.

Jacob heard the clunk of a car door opening and heavy-soled shoes strike the pavement. They were close now, and he wanted to look but didn't dare. He didn't want to give away their position. The feet moved away; another clunk and another man caused sounds of metal clinking together while heavy feet slapped the pavement. Jacob listened to the sounds of the doors slamming shut.

Murphy didn't move. Jacob could feel Stephens behind him, lying almost on the back of his legs and could hear the soldier breathing. Suddenly Murphy rose up to a kneeling position all the while concealed in the high grass and the cover of dark. Stephens slowly crawled past Jacob and rose up next to Murphy. Jacob remained lying in the grass, not wanting to move as the two soldiers set out ahead, walking much faster now while still crouched in the grass.

Frustrated and not wanting to be left behind, Jacob lifted himself to a push-up position and brought his knees forward. He climbed up and followed the other two. He could see the patrol car clearly now. It was empty. Whoever previously occupied it was gone. Murphy and Stephens moved quickly along the shoulder, then cut diagonally across the pavement and crouched near the patrol driver's side door. Jacob knelt by the brush guard at the hood of the car while Murphy circled it, and Stephens moved around to the passenger side to look through the window.

"Keys are in it," Stephens whispered just as they heard heavy shoes striking pavement in the distance and moving back in their direction.

Jacob ducked behind the grill of the patrol car. Without speaking, Stephens and Murphy moved back to flank him, where they watched and waited. As the footsteps grew louder, Murphy stood straight up, holding his rifle in front of him, the stock in his shoulder and the barrel still pointed down at the street. Stephens did the same, side stepping and using the vehicle for cover. Stephens looked down at Jacob cowering. "Stand up fool; get your weapon out," he hissed under his breath. "And be ready, just in case."

Jacob forced himself to his feet and raised the small rifle in the direction of the footsteps just as two figures emerged from the shadows. Both were police officers wearing black body armor; one cradled a shotgun, the other walked with an empty holster. They continued moving forward, then stopped as they saw the trio formed up around the patrol car. The officers didn't speak, or even as much as look at each other to communicate.

Their movements were jerky. One stepped awkwardly to the left, trying to focus on them while the one with the shotgun took a quick step forward and brought the weapon up in his arms.

"Stop; we're with the Army," Murphy said in a commanding voice just loud enough to be heard.

Without any warning, the unarmed officer ran at Stephens, a scream erupting from the man's mouth.

Frightened, Jacob stepped back as the other officer raised the shotgun and fired. Jacob could hear and feel the buckshot zip past his head. In tandem, Stephens and Murphy brought up their weapons and fired. Jacob watched the soldiers' rounds tear holes through the officers' vests. The policemen dropped to the ground dead; the shotgun clacked as it hit the pavement.

"What the hell was that?" Stephens said, moving forward and kicking the weapon away.

Jacob quickly rounded the vehicle where Murphy was already leaning over one of the officers.

"Holy shit, you guys just killed two cops!" Jacob said.

Murphy looked back at him shaking his head. "I don't think so," he said, lifting his gloved hand. The black oily blood clung to his fingers and dripped off in thick strings, like heavy paint.

Stephens pulled out a knife and cut a long gash down the other officer's arm.

"No! Ahh, what the hell are you doing?" Jacob gasped in disgust.

The skin split open, revealing a dark oozing gelatinized flesh. "Yeah, these ain't cops. We gotta get the fuck outta here, Sergeant."

Hearing the sound of tree limbs snapping, Jacob turned his head toward the woods. More were coming, obviously attracted by the sound of gunfire.

"I said we gotta go," Stephens repeated as he ran back to the patrol car.

Jacob turned and ran after him. Stephens was already in the driver's side with the car running before Jacob jumped into the backseat. The passenger's door closed with Murphy slapping the dash and yelling. "Go, go, go!"

Stephens hit the gas, the tires spun, and the car pulled away before the first of them broke the tree line. Jacob watched out of the passenger's window as several of them ran onto the road and turned to follow the patrol car. They passed abandoned cars rolled to the sides of the road, houses with broken windows and doors left to hang open, and the occasional abandoned body on a sidewalk. Stephens drove at high speed with the lights off until he hit a side street and quickly slowed to make the turn in time, the engine roaring with every maneuver. He drove for several more minutes, pulled to the curb of an empty road, coasted to a stop, and cut the engine.

Jacob looked out and knew they were only blocks from the park. There were no homes here; it was a long, empty street. A river ran parallel to the road on the left and he knew they would cross a bridge ahead that would take them to the park's main gate. To the right stood a high "noise pollution" fence that sheltered the high-priced homes on the other side from the traffic sounds.

Stephens pressed a button, and the cars doors all locked simultaneously. "Looks like a nice enough neighborhood, but why take any chances." He grabbed the CB radio, clicked the mic, and scanned through all of the channels only to receive interference and static. "Nothing; we can't get our comms on this radio without the frequencies loaded. Cops must be off the net," he said, clicking it off and letting the mic hit the floor.

"What the hell happened back there?" Jacob asked.

Murphy looked at him over the backseat. "I'd say we got away. Were you hit?"

"No, I wasn't hit... but he shot at us!"

"Yeah, they do that sometimes," Stephens whispered. Keeping his hands on the steering wheel, he continued looking straight ahead.

"What do you mean, they do that sometimes?" Jacob asked, frustrated.

Stephens shook his head and leaned back in the seat. "It's like some of them know. Like if they was cops, they keep doing cop shit. They get smarter the longer they're out there. I've seen soldiers still holding their rifles and walking patrol while surrounded by more of the darkness. Carpenters holding hammers. Butchers with knives. Most of 'em are like what we saw back there, you know... like zombies or something, but sometimes... yeah, sometimes they shoot at us."

Stephens let out a long sigh. "But I don't think they want to kill us," he said. "I think they want to take us; you notice they leave the people they kill? It's only the living they keep, and their own dead."

"Why do you think they do that? What do they want?" Jacob asked.

"Us," Murphy said, turning back and looking ahead to stare out the windshield. "They want to replace us."

"You guys have lost it," Jacob said looking away; he knew they were right, but he wasn't ready to accept it. "What are we doing here? Why aren't we going to the park?"

"Too dangerous," Stephens said. "We approach at night and the guards will light us up."

"So we just flash the lights or something… so they know we're normal," Jacob suggested.

"Bro, you ain't fucking getting it! The darkness has lights too. They have everything we have; the only way to know the difference is to get up close. You gotta see the shit in their eyes, man. Most of 'em scream and run at you, but some—like those cops back there—those ones will wait until they're close before they show any sign. No, we can't go to the park tonight. The park don't allow any traffic in or out after dark anyway."

Jacob sat back looking at his feet. He looked back up at the soldiers in the front seat.

"This isn't happening; it can't be."

"Oh, it's happening, Jacob. It's happening everywhere," Murphy whispered.

"Everywhere?" Jacob asked.

Murphy reached down and clicked on the car's FM radio. It scanned over several stations before hitting on one, another public service announcement in a monotone voice warning people to stay indoors. Murphy pressed the scan button again. The FM dial scanned and hit more stations all relaying the same sort of recorded messages— government spokesmen and small town officials reading prepared statements of little facts and false promises. Murphy switched to AM, skipped ahead, and stopped on a solemn man's voice.

"We're all in a bad way, folks. Judgment day is here. Satan's army is marching on the White House as we speak. There is still time to repent, people. Won't you pray with me?"

Murphy hit the button again. The digital numbers scrolled by and stopped. A man was speaking calmly and reading a list of names, one after another, in a steady cadence.

"Davis, Martin, 4. Jones, Douglas, 3, Roberts, Alice, alone."

"What is he talking about?" Jacob asked, speaking over the narrator.

"Those are the families evacuated; the name of the sponsor and number of family members," Stephens answered. "With no phones, it's the only way to get the word out."

"Riley, Steven 3, Marcus, Joseph, 2, Silvas, Richard, 2."

"Evacuated where? The park? Is that where they took my family?"

"No; the list comes from north of here in Chicago. They're taking the ferries out on Lake Michigan," Murphy said.

"Ferries? No way, too many people," Jacob said.

Murphy sighed and shook his head. He opened a leather tool bag on the floor of the patrol car and found two boxes of 12-gauge shells. He opened the box and started reloading the shotgun he'd recovered from the dead officer.

"Was… too many people; not anymore." Murphy pressed the scan button again, finding a station just as a fatigued voice was giving a graphic content warning to the listening audience. The broadcaster's voice faded to a recording filled with static and crackles of background noise. A reporter was on the street, in the middle of chaos.

Jacob listened to the man breathing rapidly as he ran, the microphone clicking and banging off of objects. He heard the man tumble, and the mic went dead with a loud crack before clacking back to life.

"This is real; they are firing on us right now! Remnants of the Army National Guard are firing on our position. I repeat… members on the Illinois National Guard have joined the protestors and are shooting at us! Whoever—whatever—they are, they are advancing! I don't know how much longer I can report on this channel…" The microphone again faded in and out as gunfire erupted around the reporter's position. The sounds seemed to swallow the man's voice.

"If anyone is listening, we are located at Northerly Island. State Police and the Chicago Police Department are here, but we need your help. You can't hide anymore; you need to fight. Get out of your homes and come to Northerly Island. Come to the Castle and bring any weapons you have…" More sounds of automatic gunfire and explosions drowned out the recording and suddenly the sound went to static. The broadcaster was back but Murphy reached over and shut off the radio.

"It's like this everywhere. It started small, with the riots, and now it's come to this," Murphy whispered. "When they called me up, they said it was for riot duty downtown—we didn't last more than a day. We were stupid; we came rolling into town in our trucks. We put up yellow tape and wooden barriers, like it was some kind of peaceful protest. At first they ignored the barricades and stayed away from the roadblocks; then we watched them take down pedestrians and the weak right in front of our eyes. They ignored us, just staying far enough away so that we couldn't stop them. We were ordered to hold, to contain the line… that the police were supposed to do the arresting.

"After dark, they started to bunch up together. Their numbers had multiplied. Suddenly they came at us—not trying to get past us—they actually wanted us! They would reach through the shields and snatch people. They'd pull someone back, and they'd pass them deeper into the mob like a baton. I watched many of my own men dragged off, and there was nothing I could do to help them. The normal stuff didn't work. Tear gas, rubber bullets. Sure, fire hoses knocked them down, but didn't stop 'em.

"We fought hard, but we couldn't hold them back. By dawn, we were using lethal ammo… but they still came. We… we were killing them by the hundreds, but they still came and grabbed us."

Murphy pressed back against the seat and took a long drink of water from his drinking tube. He let out a long sigh. "Just before dawn, orders came to pull back. We loaded up in the trucks and prepared to move out, but…"

"But what?" Jacob asked.

"I saw them," Murphy whispered.

Stephens nodded. "I know, brother. I saw it too; we all did."

"What? What did you see?" Jacob asked impatiently.

"The soldiers—the ones we lost, our friends. They were back but changed… still wearing their riot gear. They marched with the mobs," Murphy said.

Jacob leaned back in the seat. "This is all bullshit. It had to have been something else. Maybe another unit, a group you didn't know about, in stolen uniforms."

Murphy nodded and turned his head to look out the window. "Yeah, maybe you're right."

Stephens started the car's engine and put it into gear. "We need a place to hole up."

Chapter 10

The patrol car rolled slowly down the center of the empty road as Jacob surveyed the small industrial park that was coming up on their left side. Only a block from the two-lane road that led to the park encampment, it would make for a perfect hide.

Stephens slowed the car until it was rolling just above idle speed, then turned into a paved drive that faced a building with a double overhead door. The wheels crunched as the car maneuvered over broken asphalt. A large sign at the front of the building labeled it a commercial heating and cooling sales shop. Stephens eased the patrol car forward, then stopped it in front of the door—close, but not so close that he couldn't turn and flee if need be—then reached down and shut off the ignition.

"Why here?" Jacob whispered, still frustrated they were not going straight to the park. He was growing anxious with worry about his family.

"This building looks solid enough: only one door in the front, no windows, steel overheads," Stephens listed off patiently as he dropped his arm and secured his rifle. He reached up, popped the dome light cover, and removed the bulb. He held a hand on the door and used his other to slowly pull the latch so that the door quietly released under pressure while Murphy did the same on the passenger's side.

Jacob waited and watched as they quietly let their doors swing shut. Stephens opened the back door, and Jacob realized for the first time that there were no handles on the inside of the rear passenger's doors. Stephens handed Jacob the shotgun they'd retrieved from the dead cop. "Here take this; it'll get you farther than that rifle," he said.

Jacob nodded his acceptance and stepped out of the car.

Stephens moved to the rear of the car and used the key to open the trunk. A large black gear bag was inside; Murphy reached in and opened the zipper.

Inside were a police carbine and a black tactical vest already loaded with three, thirty-round magazines. Murphy removed the rifle and set it to the side, then pulled out the heavy vest and placed it next to the rifle. The rest of the bag was filled with road flares, a protective mask, and a baton. Another bag was filled with tools and other emergency gear. Murphy closed the bags and pushed them aside. Searching the rest of the trunk, he found nothing further of use.

He waved Jacob forward and placed the vest in his hands. It was heavy. Police was stenciled across the back in white, bold letters, and an embroidered badge patch was affixed to the front center. Several loops held zip ties and other bits of equipment. Jacob pulled the vest tighter and let the weight adjust in his arms. Murphy took the rifle and opened the sling, hanging it over Jacob's back.

"Come on, man; what am I, a mule?" Jacob whispered, protesting.

"Just until we get inside; then I'll show you how to put the gear on," Murphy said.

After one more sweep of the trunk, Stephens slowly lowered the lid and pressed until he heard the latch click. The soldier reached up and dropped his NODs over his eyes, then gave Murphy a thumbs up. Murphy looked at Jacob. "Just follow us in and press your back against the wall."

Jacob nodded back to the man as Murphy pulled down his own goggles and followed Stephens to the front door of the business.

Stephens moved to the right of the door with Murphy standing just behind him. He reached out an arm and felt the handle move in his hand. The door pushed in easily and glided open, staying that way. Stephens sidestepped to the lip of the door, lowered the barrel of his rifle, tapped it twice against the doorjamb, and then pulled back. The three of them silently stood, holding their breath and listening for any sound of movement.

After several agonizing minutes, Stephens stepped into the doorway and dropped into the room with Murphy close behind him. Jacob moved in quickly after and, as instructed, pushed his back to the wall and waited. Murphy reached back and closed the door, the room quickly falling pitch black. Jacob couldn't see a hand in front of his face; he pressed against the wall and began sweating while holding the heavy gear in his trembling arms.

He could hear the soldiers' footsteps as they moved deeper into the space. Their sounds of movement reflected off walls and played tricks on Jacob's mind as he tried to imagine the layout of the room. The soldiers' steps continued to move away; then, suddenly, the room flashed in bright light. Jacob squinted, pulled up a hand to shield his eyes, and heard men yelling from a loft. Jacob watched as his friends peeled off their night vision devices and raised their hands.

Bright handheld spotlights painted them in blinding beams. Armed men chaotically yelled for them to show their hands. Jacob dropped the gear and thrust up his arms. He was ordered to move forward and online with the others. Whoever held the spotlight was using it effectively; they hit Jacob right in the face with the beam, and he couldn't see anything while blinded by the light. He tried looking away but found it impossible to escape the beam. Jacob stepped forward, nearly bumping into Murphy who was speaking low, trying to identify himself to the unknown men in the loft.

Jacob heard boots clank as they ran down a set of metal stairs. The other men continued to order them to keep their arms up. A man approached, pushing a barrel into Jacob's chest and yelled for him to look straight ahead and open his eyes and mouth. Jacob struggled to peel open his eyes against the blinding light. He heard the man yell, "Clear!"

The lights' beams were directed away and shut off. Small portable lanterns filled the room with a softer glow. A man in jeans and a Carhartt work coat stepped forward. He held a military-looking rifle in his arms and a revolver was tucked into his waistband.

He looked Jacob over and moved to the soldiers as more men, still holding their weapons on them, walked down the stairs.

"Where in the hell did you all come from?" the man asked.

Murphy began to speak, but the man held up his hand and pointed at Jacob. "Nope, I'm asking him."

"Why me?" Jacob asked.

"Cause one thing here ain't like the others and you probably ain't as good at lying. Now where did you come from?" the man asked again, stepping closer.

Jacob looked over at Murphy. The man, growing annoyed, said, "You don't need his help. Now where are you from? If I have to ask again, I'll toss you out the door… naked."

"We came from town… a few miles from here," Jacob said.

"We were evac—" Murphy began before the man angrily raised a hand, shutting him up.

He looked back at Jacob. "Continue."

"Ah, I was at my home, the convoy came down the street picking people up, my family got on the truck, but we were attacked. I got separated from my wife and kid; these men helped me. They've been helping me."

"Where'd the cop car come from?"

Jacob looked at Murphy who stood, not speaking. He shrugged to signal Jacob to continue. "Up the road; two cops… two… of… they… we killed 'em and took it."

"What did they look like… the cops?" the man asked, pressing his face uncomfortably close to Jacob's.

"It was dark… but they had the black blood," Jacob said, stepping back and looking away.

The man reached out an arm, slapped Jacob on the shoulder, and nodded to Murphy. "Okay, fair enough; my name's Johnny and this is my shop. Sorry to be an asshole, but things have gone sideways in the last week. You're free to stay the night here, but I'm afraid I can't offer you anything."

Murphy, having heard the man out, extended his hand. "I'm Sergeant Murphy with the Illinois National Guard; this is Corporal Stephens. We're assigned to the Wilson Street Park. Have you heard anything from them?"

The man looked at Murphy with wide eyes. "You're joking, right?"

Murphy stood silently, then turned to face Jacob and Stephens and shrugged his shoulders.

The man called out in the direction of the loft behind him. "Miller, get down here."

Jacob watched as a younger man dressed in an identical Carhartt jacket ran down the stairs, taking them two at a time. He stopped just short of Johnny.

"These two say they're stationed at the Wilson Street Park," Johnny said.

Miller shook his head. "Shit no, they gone. Pulled out this evening—shit-load of trucks, tanks, helicopters… everything. That camp they built is empty," Miller said. "I watched 'em leave with my own eyes."

Stephens clenched his fist angrily and swiped at the air. "Dammit! The jump order must've come down and we missed it!"

"What does that mean?" Jacob said, panicking. "Where the hell did they go? Where is my family?"

"It means we're fucked," Stephens said, disgusted.

Murphy turned to face the younger man who had come down from the loft. "Miller is it? How do you know this?"

"I was there when they left, moved off to the big evacuation point. I came back here to stay with Uncle Johnny; we're waiting on my dad and some others. The soldiers said they were pulling back to the lake front."

"Northerly Island," Jacob mumbled, feeling lightheaded.

"Yeah, how'd you know?" Miller answered, looking Jacob up and down. "Hey man, are you hurt? Your leg's all bloody. You don't look so good."

Jacob suddenly felt far away and unable to answer—despair, exhaustion, and worry for his family taking a hard toll. He just stared at Miller, watching him talk. Jacob could see that the young man's lips were moving, but he no longer heard the words. Stephens moved between the other men to look at the wound on Jacob's hip.

"Dammit, fool, you let this get to bleeding again. Now I'm going to have to re-dress it," Stephens said as Jacob began leaning forward, so far that Stephens had to catch and steady him. Wearily, Jacob watched through clouding vision as Johnny tilted his head to look at the nasty blood-soaked bandages coming loose from Jacob's side. He grimaced and turned to Murphy. "Why don't you get him upstairs; there's more people up there. They can help with that." Jacob closed his eyes as the man continued to speak.

Chapter 11

Jacob didn't know how long he'd been out; he didn't remember being moved to the bed or even lying down. He looked across the darkened floor space; the long, narrow room was lit only by a few candles. Heavy machinery was interspersed with moving lumps of blanket on the floors and tired men holding rifles, keeping watch over their families as they leaned against walls. A child cried from some place in the back. A sharp pain pulling at the wound in his hip caused him to turn away. He jerked to the side to look back and saw a woman cleaning his wound with a damp wad of gauze.

"Oh, you're awake," she whispered.

Jacob squinted, trying to see her face in the low light. He could make out that she was middle aged, her hair was pulled back, and she wore a dark sweater. He tried to sit up for a better look but the weight of his own body prevented it.

The woman placed a hand on his chest and eased him back onto the cot. "Come on now, hun, you need to rest. Just let me get this bandaged for you," she whispered.

"Where am I?'

She pushed a gauze dressing around the wound. Holding it in place, she attached a long piece of tape. "You're in the loft of the shop. You got a little dizzy down there, and your friends brought you up here."

"Where are they?"

"They're here; don't worry, they didn't leave you," she whispered, pulling a blanket over his lap.

A loud rumble from overhead shook and vibrated the corrugated roofing above their heads. Jacob jumped and tried to sit up. Again, the nurse gracefully lowered him to his back. "It's okay; just relax."

"What was that?" Jacob asked, the shock obvious in his voice.

"I was told it's the Air Force dropping their bombs in town," the nurse answered.

"Bombing? But... I thought they were evacuating everyone."

Rumbling explosions in the distance shook the building, the air cracking with impacts.

The clanking of footsteps came up the stairs, followed by the smiling face of Stephens, who overheard the last bits of the conversation. "They're CAS missions," Stephens said, moving to Jacob's side. "How you feeling?"

"CAS?" Jacobs asked.

"Close air support."

Not understanding, Jacob looked blankly at him as aircraft flew low overhead, on another pass.

"They're blowing the hell out of the things trying to get close to our people!" Stephens said over the very distant rumblings of explosions, a remote and deadly fireworks display ripping apart the night air. "Those are Warthogs, most likely. I'd say they're pulling out all the stops tonight. About damn time too."

Jacob shook his head. "Why didn't you just say that to start with?"

"That is what I said; not my fault you don't understand shit."

The crack, crack, crack of gunfire echoed from somewhere outside the building—far away at first but quickly moving closer. Stephens stepped back and ran to the loft window overlooking the factory floor. Jacob pushed himself to a seated position, this time ignoring the nurse's advice. The gunfire grew louder and was joined by the ping and squeal of rounds slapping against the building's metal skin. Stephens turned and walked hurriedly for the stairs leading to the factory floor as hidden faces in the loft began to cry out and speak in hushed tones.

Jacob sat upright and slipped his pants on halfway before he searched the floor at his feet in the dim candlelight. He found his boots and quickly slipped them on. Giving the laces a quick yank, he wrapped them around his ankles and knotted them. He looked around and saw his shirt and jacket in a bundle at the end of the cot. He got to his feet and felt the pull at his side, his hand instinctively dropping.

He pulled his pants up the rest of the way over the bandage and winced at the discomfort.

The nurse, watching him with frustration, moved and grabbed his shirt and jacket. "I had to stitch you up. Sorry, I only had a local anesthetic and not much for the pain; it will be wearing off soon," she said hurriedly as she helped Jacob into his jacket. "You'll need to have that cleaned again and the stitches out in a week or so."

Jacob nodded and searched the jacket pockets and the empty holster on his waist. "Where are my guns?" he gasped.

The woman moved along the wall just behind the cot to a tall metal cabinet. She quickly returned, carrying the black tactical vest and police carbine. Jacob noticed at once that his P89 was now fastened into a holster on the chest of the vest. "This is yours. The soldiers said you would gladly trade the other rifle and shotgun for the medicine we used on you," she said, placing the rifle on the bed and handing Jacob the vest.

The vest was open at the sides, but he'd never worn one before. He stuck his head through the center, nearly getting lost in the heavy armor. The nurse stepped in and pulled the Velcro side apart and snugged the vest down over him, then lashed the Velcro waist straps.

"You aren't too familiar with this, are you?" she said, helping him to adjust the straps.

"No, guess I never had much reason to put one on before tonight."

She curled her brow, throwing Jacob a puzzled look. "Well, this is correct. Unfortunately, I have spent enough time in the ER to know how an officer's gear goes on and off."

Jacob nodded a thank you as he looked over the snaps and attachments at the front of the vest. He tried pulling them until he felt the pressure against his wound. The heavy plates in the chest and back caused the other straps to cut into his shoulders. He lifted himself to his feet and shrugged hard, trying to adjust the weight before he took an uneven step toward the stairs.

"Officer, your gun!" the nurse called after him. She moved toward him, holding the rifle.

Jacob turned to look at her, and then recalled seeing an embroidered badge patch on the front of the tactical vest. Suddenly, he realized that the entire time, she had assumed he was a police officer. "I'm not a—oh, right. Thanks."

He paused then reached out for the rifle. Never having really held one like this before, it was foreign in his grip. A magazine that stuck out of the lower receiver was already seated, so Jacob let his hands work over the metal and up the handguards to feel the weight of the rifle. He turned it to the sides, examining the mechanisms. Pushing a button, the magazine dropped and nearly fell to the floor before he clumsily caught it and slapped it back home.

Mistaking Jacob's curiosity with the new weapon as an inspection, the nurse said, "It's fine; nobody messed with it."

Jacob thanked her and walked toward the stairs, spotting families hiding in the shadows of the loft as he passed them. He turned into the opening and clanged down the metal treads to the factory floor.

The lower level was dark with all the lights off, and rounds continued to ping off the outer walls. Jacob was able to spot Murphy and Stephens pressed against the door they'd entered earlier. Johnny, along with some of his own men, was crowded around them while Murphy was trying to convince Johnny to move his people away—and losing the argument. Murphy turned his head, catching the movement of Jacob's approach.

"What are you doing down here?" Murphy asked. "You're going to bust yourself open and start bleeding again."

Jacob stepped closer to the group, holding the rifle awkwardly in his hands. "You need everyone," Jacob said just above a whisper, the fear showing in his voice as the sounds of battle echoed just beyond the walls.

"You even know how to use that?" Murphy asked, reaching out and snatching the rifle from Jacob's hands. He dropped the magazine then reseated it. He instructed Jacob, giving a quick rundown of the rifle's parts and functions. He pulled back the charging handle and chambered a round before turning the rifle so that Jacob could see the selector switch. "This is safe, that's semi… don't even fuck with the other one." Then he pushed the rifle back into Jacob's hand.

"Stay here with them; we're going outside to see what's going on. If we breakout, we'll come back for you and the others," Murphy ordered.

Jacob shook his head. "No, I'm sticking with you."

Stephens turned and faced Murphy. "Come on, Sergeant; he's just going to slow us down," Jacob overheard him whisper.

Murphy looked at Jacob waiting eagerly as rounds stitched the top of the building and a loud explosion rattled the steel sides. Murphy dropped his head, rubbed his temple with his gloved hand, and then forced a grin. "Fine, get your ass behind Stephens and don't miss." Murphy turned to Johnny. "Take care of your people. If I can get contact with my command, we'll send someone back for you."

Johnny nodded, reaching toward the door's handle. "Good luck out there," he said, slapping Murphy on the back as the door swung open. Murphy looked back over his shoulder and cut out into the night with Stephens following close. Jacob lurched forward and hesitated in the doorway. He felt a nudge from behind as he was shoved outside, and the door closed behind him.

Murphy and Stephens were running, crouched between the patrol car and the building. Jacob came to his senses and took off after them, sprinting as more gunfire erupted from close by. Murphy rounded the far side of the car, dropped to a prone position, and crawled to the rear bumper. Stephens squatted, keeping the engine block between himself and the sounds of battle. Jacob ran and dropped in next to him.

He looked out at the field across the street. It was dark, and he couldn't make out any figures— only the muzzles of weapons spitting flame as they fired. Tracers cut back and forth across the field and occasional rounds flew over Jacob's head, smacking into the steel-clad building behind him. Jacob looked to his left and saw Stephens hovered over his rifle with his night vision down. Murphy scooted back away from the tire and rejoined them around the hood.

"Looks like a patrol made contact," Murphy whispered, "They're taking some heavy fire from the tree line. I think if we target them from here, it'll loosen up their flank."

"You sure, Sergeant? They don't even know we're up here. What if our guys fire on us?" Stephens protested, not looking up from his rifle.

Jacob looked around. He was still blind in the dark but could hear the sustained battle coming from across the street. "What are you two talking about?"

Murphy grinned. "There's a unit in the field over there. Someone… something has them pinned; we're gonna suppress so they can maneuver."

Jacob scowled. "Just tell me what to do."

"That's the spirit. Let's go; we need to get distance on this building. We don't want to draw attention to it."

Chapter 12

Jacob sat anxiously behind the wheel of the patrol car. He had the vehicle in neutral as the soldiers pushed it out of the factory's parking lot and into the street. The car slowly rolled back, entered the decline, and picked up speed. The two soldiers jogged to keep up. Jacob maneuvered the car backwards and into the street. He overcut the wheel, causing the car to turn too far and smack into the curb, one tire screeching against it as the steel rim impacted the concrete.

Murphy ran up alongside the driver's window. "Okay; when I give the word, start the car and hit the field with your high beams."

Jacob looked through the windshield to the field in front of him where he could still see the muzzle flashes and the tracer fire crisscrossing the dark sky like laser beams.

"How will they know we are the good guys?" Jacob asked nervously.

"Don't worry. Soon as I drain a mag into those black-eyed monsters, they'll know who we're siding up with," Stephens said, moving close to the car and leaning his rifle over its roof.

"Do it," Murphy ordered, speaking louder.

Jacob felt the key in the ignition and turned on the engine; it quickly roared to life.

"Hit the lights!" Murphy yelled.

Jacob searched the left side of the column and found the toggle. He pulled the lever, turning on the lights. He hit the switch that activated the high beams, then grabbed the hand-powered spotlight and directed it into the field. His stomach dropped and he fought the urge to run back to the factory.

The terrain to the front was filled with moving figures—men, women, and children running through the high grass toward a line of soldiers dug in on a side street. The men fired desperately, trying to hold back the approaching mass. Farther behind the swarm were more of the things, armed and indiscriminately organized. Walking straight ahead with their rifles loosely tucked into their shoulders, they shot blindly toward the soldiers on the far side of the field.

Jacob steeled his nerves and pointed the spotlight at the things in the open, causing their dark eyes to turn in his direction. Murphy's rifle rattled off a burst and Stephens' quickly joined it. The target direction for the creatures changed as they turned ninety degrees and headed for the road. As Murphy predicted, this now had the swarm moving perpendicular to the line of soldiers in the field and allowed them to shoot at the sides of the mob, more effectively cutting them down.

A round smacked the windshield and Jacob ducked down. When he rose back up, he saw a statue-like man aiming a rifle in his direction. Jacob moved the spotlight to blind him while rounds pecked around the man's feet before one found home and knocked him back. Jacob continued to move the light, pointing out targets and blinding the rushing things as they moved across the high grass. As Jacob directed the light, he saw that the approaching waves were thinning out. The things on the fringes with weapons disappeared back into the shadows while anything alive in the field was being cut down by the soldiers on the side street.

The passenger's door opened and Stephens dropped into the seat, quickly changing out magazines in his weapon. He rolled down the window and fired again while leaning out. Murphy smashed out the rear window then jumped in the back. Reaching across, he kicked out the other side and slapped the cage with a gloved hand. "Okay, let's move. Get up to that side street where the troopers are. Drive slow; I'm sure they're a bit jumpy… and cut off the spotlight."

"What's all the window breaking about?" Jacob asked.

"Windows and doors don't open back here; I don't want to get trapped," Murphy said.

Jacob powered down the directional light and locked the car into gear. He drove ahead cautiously while Stephens occasionally took shots from the passenger's window, cutting down stragglers that were still moving. Drawing closer to the side street, men in uniform ran forward and shot hand signals to

Jacob. He saw the palm of a soldier's hand and the business end of a light machine gun.

"Cut the lights, stop, and put it in park," Murphy said.

Jacob reached down turned off the headlights, as instructed. He saw Stephens looking straight ahead through his goggles. He held open the passenger's door, slowly stepped out, and walked straight ahead. He turned back and pointed toward the car. Murphy exited, took steps forward just past the bumper, and then moved back to the driver's window.

"Okay, kill the engine and get out," Murphy ordered. "Follow me."

Jacob shut off the car and reached between the seats, grabbing his rifle. Leaving the keys in the ignition, he joined Murphy in the street. The soldier led them ahead in the dark toward a group of men sheltered at the rear of an old bread truck resting on flat tires. A man held a red-lens flashlight to cast a soft red glow over a group of kneeling soldiers examining a map. Jacob suddenly noticed they weren't walking alone; they were being escorted by two soldiers in full gear. As they approached the gathering around the map, a rugged man in uniform stood and looked them up and down. Old and grizzled with tanned leather skin, Jacob could tell by the way he carried himself that he was in charge.

He stepped away from the group and walked over to them. "Thanks for the support back there.

Who are you with?" the man said just above a whisper.

"Sergeant Murphy, 38th MP, Illinois National Guard. You?" Murphy said.

"First Sergeant Bowe, 420th Engineer Battalion, out of Gary; I thought all you Natty boys were cleared out of here," the man said. "My command element is about a block south if that's what you're looking for."

"First Sergeant, we got some survivors held up in the warehouse down the street," Murphy said.

Bowe stopped and turned to shout orders to the group of soldiers gathered to his rear. "Okay, we can take care of that; now what are you all doing here? Where's the rest of your unit?"

"We need a route to the north. We got hit on an evac run and got separated from the rest of the 38th. What's going on here, First Sergeant?" Murphy asked.

Bowe turned and pointed an arm up and down the road. Adjusting to the natural light, Jacob could now make out shapes in the distance. All along the road going away from him, soldiers were dug into the shoulder and facing west. Jacob turned and saw more of them beyond the main road leading all the way to the river and past the factory.

"We just moved up here in the last half hour; been pushing our way west all day. Higher ups finally got their heads out of their asses—this is a full-on containment zone now. We've been tasked to hold sixteen city blocks. No easy feat. The Zoomies started dropping lots of ordnances in the town out there; not sure what good it does, but after every run, we get a load of 'em headed this way. Poking the hornets' nest."

"Are you going into the town? Are there still survivors there?" Jacob asked.

Bowe paused to stare at Jacob; with a clenched jaw, he let out a guttural sound that made Jacob fear the man might bark. "What? Well, civvy, right now what we have is a defensive line going south to the interstate and north to the 2nd Street Bridge; beyond that, it goes right up to Lake Michigan."

"What about the people at the park? Where are they?" Jacob blurted out.

"You a cop?" the first sergeant asked, looking at Jacob's vest.

Ignoring the question, Jacob asked again, "Do you know where they went?"

Murphy put a hand on Jacob's shoulder. "First Sergeant, we were extracting his family; we were en-route to the park when we got cut off. Do you know where they moved to?"

"Folks at the park are gone; all the civilians are either being pushed south toward Kentucky or up onto the ferries on Lake Michigan. If they moved this afternoon, I'd guess they shot straight up to Northerly Island."

"That's it, the island. That's what was on the radio, what Miller told us," Jacob said.

"Well, if you want to go there, you better get moving. They're closing the corridor in forty-eight hours. Shit, most of it's probably already collapsed. You'll have to head straight up this route; the main highways are all blocked. The Seabees were running the route clearance missions with the Marines and keeping it open, but that was before these things started shooting back.

"Every hour, they get a bit smarter. Hell, I heard over the company net they're starting to set up ambushes, blocking the roads and sniping from cover. Even some of these human wave attacks are letting up—like they're improving their tactics."

"They're smarter? Like how…? Do we even know what they are?" Murphy asked.

Bowe squinted. "You mean The Darkness? Fuck if I know what they are. HQ is calling it an invasion… I ain't kidding; that's the words they used. Not outbreak, not riot control. They said invasion. Craziest shit I ever seen—like Fallujah all over again, except these things don't get scared.

"Most units have pulled back to this defensive line, letting the Air Force cut them down. Urban search and rescue has been called off for anything in the city limits or west of this position." Bowe paused and looked intently at Murphy. "Could I give you a bit of advice?"

Murphy looked at Jacob, then back at the first sergeant. "I'm afraid I already know what you're going to say."

Bowe reached into his pocket and removed a tin of tobacco. He smacked it against his palm then opened the lid, stuffing a bit under his lip. "I think you should stick with us; the Lake Michigan route is all but closed. Northerly isn't going to hold much longer either. If you got family up there, you aren't going to do them any good getting yourself and these men killed," he said, looking at Jacob. "Only about sixty percent of the boys showed up for the recall; I'm shorthanded so we could use your help."

"I have to get to my family," Jacob said adamantly.

"I get it; I really do, but the routes are closing up. I'm not sure you understand the gravity of the situation," Bowe said, pointing out over the now empty fields. The sky was lit with blooms of orange and yellow as bombs exploded far in the distance while the sounds of remote gunfire echoed through the trees.

Jacob ignored the first sergeant and looked at Murphy. "I'll just take the car and go on alone."

"Hold up; nobody is going anywhere alone," Murphy said, raising his hand.

Stephens shook his head and started to walk away before stopping and looking back. "You should let him go, Sergeant; this isn't our mission anymore."

Murphy laughed. "This isn't for him. We have orders and vital intel; we need to link back up with Battalion. If they headed north to the city then that's where I'm going. I understand if you want to hang back here with these guys, Stephens; no hard feelings."

Stephens looked disgusted. He stomped away a few paces and cussed, then stopped and came back. "Man, this is some bull-shit!"

Bowe looked at Murphy and chuckled. "Well, I guess I owe you one for the help you gave me back there. If you insist on going, I can at least get you resupplied."

Chapter 13

Jacob laid his head back on the bench seat of the patrol car. Stephens was driving tactically with the lights off. His helmet was on the seat and he navigated by sparse moonlight. Going so slow and stopping so frequently, they were often passed by soldiers speed walking up the road or held up by crowds of wandering refugees being pushed south. Stephens had to keep the car to the far right, as the left lane of the road was lined with soldiers. Occasionally, they'd pass a roadblock where men would stop the vehicle and shine lights in their mouths and eyes before allowing them to pass.

Jacob leaned back in the seat and observed the men outside his window as the car passed them. Every so often a machine gun would fire a long burst into the far-off tree lines or at an object on a distant street. At one point, they drove by a large group of field artillery firing barrages into the city skyline. The firing of the big cannons rocked the car and made the windows vibrate.

At other parts of the road, it was quiet, only occupied by tired soldiers in work parties building fortifications against the things to the west. Who those things were still hadn't been explained; Jacob heard most soldiers refer to them as "The Darkness". He saw the dried and shriveled corpses stacked and piled like cordwood at points on the road—no respect being paid to the bodies of whatever they had become.

Looking to the distance from the passenger's window, he could see tall pillars of smoke rising above the trees. The neighborhoods west of the highway were now burning, the fires caused by the relentless bombing that was ordered through the night in an attempt to hold back "The Darkness". On the seat beside him sat a large nylon backpack that at one time held chemical gear. Under Bowe's orders, the supply sergeant near Johnny's shop had dumped the bag out and packed it with loaded magazines for Jacob's rifle.

He had also stuffed in a couple bottles of water, an old flashlight, and a few of the bagged meals like the one Murphy had shared earlier. Jacob had read everything on the package after the supply sergeant handed the MREs to him. The meager things in the nylon bag were all Jacob owned now; everything he had before was back in the house—the house that's probably long gone, burnt to the ground, nothing but splinters and ash. Is this my new life?

The car stopped abruptly and a bright flashlight shined through the window. A soldier kept the light on Stephens as a second man approached from the shadows and probed the passengers with a light of his own.

"End of the line, gentlemen. Mouths open," he ordered, crouching so that he could see inside the patrol car.

Jacob looked straight at the light and held his mouth open; the soldier scanned their faces then clicked off the light. "What's with the wheels?" he asked.

"It's a loaner; the Bentley's in the shop," Stephens answered.

"Okay, smart ass; what are you doing this far north?"

Murphy leaned forward so that he could see the soldier. "Moving to Northerly, trying to link up with the 33rd."

The soldier yelled to the other one holding the light. The light cut off as the second soldier ran away to a Humvee on the side of the road and then came running back with a clipboard. He handed the board off to the man at the window. The solider lifted up the pages, quickly flipping them over the top of the board, and stopped near the bottom. He looked back up at Murphy.

"The 33rd?"

Murphy nodded. "Yeah, that's right."

"Well, they came through late afternoon. I got their manifest right here; but hell, the route's closed up now."

Jacob reached for the handle through the broken window, opened his door, and stepped into the street before reaching for the clipboard. "You have a manifest?"

The soldier pulled away, his hand dropping to his sidearm. "Whoa, back up now! Who are you?" the man said, taking a defensive stance. The second soldier quickly came back into view and put the light in Jacob's face.

"Dammit, will you cut that shit out? I just want to see if my family was on the list!"

The soldier lowered the light so it shone on Jacob's chest as the first man looked down at the clipboard, then at Jacob sympathetically. "Names?"

"Laura Anderson, Katy Anderson," Jacob said.

The soldier unfolded a long, tri-folded paper log sheet. "Gimme some light," he said as his finger ran down a list of names from top to bottom. "Oh, here we go, Laura Anderson, 2 members."

Jacob leaned forward. Looking at the handwritten entry, he smiled. "So they're at the Island then?"

"Now, I didn't say that. I'm just saying they came by here."

"Okay, thank you." Jacob's hand dropped to the door handle.

The soldier put out his arm, resting it at the top of the door. "Hold up; like I said, the route is closed now. It collapsed about a quarter mile north of here. Closed all the way up to Museum Park. I'm sorry; I'm going to have to turn you around. That's no man's land up ahead."

Jacob stepped forward to the barrier and looked into the dark landscape beyond the roadblock. They were beside an old brick fire station that sat just beyond them to the right. The building's walls were now reinforced with sandbags going up nearly five feet. Concrete forms in a serpentine pattern with wooden sawhorses blocked the road ahead; a hastily erected sandbag bunker was positioned to guard the approach.

Jacob looked off into the distance, seeing no movement. The terrain no longer held green residential neighborhoods. To the left, was a sparsely wooded lot and less than a hundred feet ahead from where he stood, a steel-girded bridge met the road. Jacob turned back toward the car where Murphy and Stephens were now standing near the gate guards. "How far to the museum?" he asked.

"Shit, might as well be a thousand miles tonight," one of the men said.

Jacob turned and glared at them. The first soldier came forward and looked out across the bridge. "It's a good twenty miles, sir—but it's really bad. The marines pulled back a couple hours ago and, hell, they were in AMTRAKS."

"I don't know what that is, but I'm going," Jacob muttered, turning back to look at the bridge.

"Sorry, sir, my orders were to hold all civilians. You being a cop and all… I mean, I guess if you really need to get yourself killed tonight, nothing I can do about it. But seriously, those Marines… they were in bad shape when they came limping back. The things are changing."

"Is the road clear or not?" Jacob asked.

The soldier shook his head. "Most of the way, but it's completely blocked at the railroad. You'll have to finish up on foot—and that's through heavy areas—the museum is still under siege; you'd have to get through that and—"

Jacob watched as a hole popped at the base of the man's neck. The soldier's eyes went wide, and his left hand reached up as the echo of a single gunshot cracked. The machine gun on the Humvee opened up and flames spit from the barrel as the gunner swept the tree line with fire. Jacob was tackled from behind and pushed to the side.

"Get down, you fool!" Stephens yelled at him as he lifted his rifle and fired quick shots off into the trees.

Jacob stared at the asphalt and watched the expended brass from Stephens' rifle bounce and roll at his feet. He steadied himself and rose to a knee, keeping the concrete barrier between his body and the incoming rounds. He looked out beyond the sandbag bunker; armed men were rushing in under the cover of the trees. Unlike before, when they would run head on into incoming fire, this group would run, disappear from sight, and then rise up shooting at the men dug in on the road. Rounds smacked into the Humvee and the gunner went limp—another soldier quickly took his place.

A machine gun positioned on the roof of the fire station joined the fight. Flares launched in the sky, casting long, haunting shadows over the approaching army charging in from the woods. Jacob watched as a soldier to his left was hit; he was knocked back and looked at the hole in his armor that miraculously landed at the very center of his chest plate. The soldier put a finger in the hole, looked up at Jacob, and smiled just as a second round hit the man in the top of the head.

Jacob felt fear, then anger build in his gut. He forced his rifle up and aimed into the tree line, pulling the trigger continuously though he couldn't see his targets. He could hear a soldier speaking into a radio frantically, "Requesting fire support; unit in danger of being overrun."

Men screamed farther down the line behind them. Jacob turned as an explosion ripped through a bunker. Soon after, men dressed in civilian clothing and carrying all manner of weapons poured into the street, breeching the defensive line.

Jacob flinched at the shriek of an incoming round moments before it crashed into the far tree line and exploded, lighting the night sky. The radio operator continued yelling into the handset, "More, more, more, on target, fire for effect!"

Rounds shrieked in and began erupting all along the defensive line. Earth and smoke were tossed into the air. Murphy grabbed Jacob by the collar and pulled him back, then shoved him toward the rear seat of the patrol car. Jacob turned and looked down the road, back in the direction they'd traveled. The swarms were inside the containment zone, running and fighting the soldiers. Blood and blue smoke mixed with a flurry of arms.

"Back in the car! Back in the car!" Murphy shouted, as he shoved Jacob into the back seat. Murphy opened the front door and stood beside it while firing his weapon across the hood as Stephens leapt in the driver's side and fired up the engine. Murphy dropped into the passenger's seat just as the car began moving. Stephens drove around the serpentine path of concrete barriers, crashing through the wooden sawhorses. Looking out of the rear window as the car raced toward the iron bridge, Jacob witnessed the soldiers left behind being overwhelmed by the swarm pressing against the fire station's walls.

Tracers crisscrossed the sky while artillery rounds exploded into the street and field, churning up earth and bodies. The smoke from the rounds quickly developed a fog that mercifully blinded Jacob from the horror.

Chapter 14

The streets were dark beyond the bridge. The scent of cordite and burning garbage hung heavy in the air. No people, no animals, no movement, no structure—nothing was left untouched. They passed a still smoking, tracked vehicle. Around it, expended brass and bits of uniform covered the street. Jacob watched as Stephens concentrated his focus on navigating around the smoldering hulk, using his night vision to maintain a course north and into Chicago.

Jacob leaned against the door, his weary eyes looking out into the street and watching the abandoned homes as they passed. Sounds of battle persisted all around them. On all sides, the glow of explosions bloomed and receded in the sky. The clacking of small arms and the booming thump of mortars and artillery rounds intermingled with the sound of low-flying aircraft roaring overhead... a manmade thunderstorm that overstimulated Jacob's already fatigued brain.

"Where is everyone?" Jacob whispered.

Murphy had his window down with his rifle aimed out and at the ready. "I haven't seen shit since we crossed the bridge."

Stephens grunted. "We're in the eye of the storm. Look around; everything here is dead. The Darkness is all around us. They're out there. If we keep driving we could run right up their ass… but that ain't gonna happen."

"What?" Murphy looked away from the open window.

Stephens flicked a finger at the dashboard. "Gas; something must'a punctured the tank back there. It's bleeding out faster than it should be."

Jacob leaned up over the rear seat to look through the window in the cage. "Can we fix it?"

Stephens shrugged. "I don't know… but I'm not about to go all Mr. Good Wrench out here in the fucking open."

"Okay, find us some place to pull over," Murphy ordered.

Stephens guided the patrol car through wreckage and a twisted makeshift barrier of wooden police obstacles and plastic barrels. Dark-blue riot gear and helmets littered the street. Just ahead was a long intersection and on the northeast corner was a tall four-story brick building—two stories higher than the neighboring structures. The sidewalk in front of the building was clear. Murphy pointed it out and Stephens gingerly brought the car up to the curb, stopping just shy of the entrance.

With the car stopped and tight to the curb, he cut the engine. They sat silently, Stephens and Murphy searching the surrounding area with their night vision and the scopes on their rifles. Jacob looked through the side window at the front of the brick building. Plywood was nailed over the front lobby windows. The entry door was doubled padlocked and held shut by a large chain. A black panel was bolted to the wall with a long list of names next to white buzzer buttons.

"Think there are people in there?" Jacob whispered uneasily.

Stephens turned his head to look. "Doubt it… it's chained from the outside. Place was probably evac'd early—especially being on the main route."

Murphy lifted his rifle. "Let's get this done; this place is creeping me out," he whispered before opening the door and stepping into the street.

Jacob moved quickly and followed him out. Murphy moved to the back of the patrol car and held up, looking out in all directions. He then turned to Jacob and adjusted his rifle in his grip so that it was against his chest, pointed down and out. "Hold it like this, 'low ready'. Watch our backs; we need to grab some gear." Stephens used the keys to open the trunk and the men rummaged through the bags while Jacob watched the surrounding buildings.

Jacob looked at the luminous dial on his wristwatch. Just after 2 am—the darkest part of the night, he thought. He looked at the watch again; his wife had given it to him as a birthday gift years ago. At the time, he had discounted it; he was so used to using his smart phone for the time that he wasn't sure if he could get back to wearing a watch again—until his wife turned the watch over and showed him the inscription on the back.

My Friend, My Love, My Hero, Laura

Reciting the words in his head didn't comfort him; instead, he felt the returning sense of helplessness and panic. Jacob looked away from his watch and gripped the rifle. Knowing he needed to stay alert, he scanned the streets. "Gotta get it together for the girls," he whispered to himself.

"What?" Stephens asked, as he approached from behind. "You see something?"

"Huh? No… you find what you were looking for?"

Stephens held up a compact set of bolt cutters and a crowbar as an answer, then walked to the chained door. He moved close to the chain and waited for Murphy to move in behind him to provide cover while he worked. Jacob followed Murphy's lead and stepped to the opposite side and looked outward into the dark street.

A clank and a snap later, Jacob could hear Stephens fishing the chain through the heavy handle of the door. The door rattle and Stephens worked the handle. "Locked; just be another minute," the soldier whispered.

Jacob looked behind him and saw Stephens wedge the bar under the plywood covering the door, just enough so that he could smack the glass with the bar. The sound shattered the otherwise silent area.

"Damn, you're being noisy. Let's step it up," Murphy whispered.

"Think you can do better, Sarge?" Stephens said as he slipped his arm inside the break. A click and a clunk later, and the door was unlocked. He pulled back and stood, peeking into the open door, checking for threats. He looked back and announced, "It's open."

"What are you waiting for?" Murphy turned to cover the street. Jacob felt him pressed against him as Murphy moved backwards, pushing him inside. They closed the door behind them and relocked it. In the pitch dark of the lobby, sealed shut by the plywood, Jacob was blind again. He felt a hand grab his wrist. "Keep hold of my vest," Murphy whispered as he guided Jacob's hand to his back.

Jacob gripped the heavy fabric of the man's vest and stumbled forward, kicking objects on the floor as he was guided down a long hallway.

"Watch your step. The floor is covered with luggage, bags, and boxes of shit people left behind," Murphy whispered.

The trio continued on shuffling; the plods of their boots echoed in the silent hallway. A latch popped and Jacob recognized the sound of a door squeaking open and items on the floor sliding as the door was pulled outward, into the hallway.

"Stairs are clear," Stephens whispered back.

Jacob was led ahead and around a corner; the echo of their footsteps changed and the space now smelled of cleaning solvent. He heard the door latch behind him and a white light clicked on. Murphy had powered up a weapon-mounted flashlight and was surveying the stairwell. It was clean—the floors polished and the walls still vibrant with fresh paint.

"Place must'a had power when they were pulled out... probably used the elevators," Stephens said. He reached into his cargo pocket and pulled out a long length of chain he'd salvaged from the front doors. He looped it through a pull handle and secured the other end to a handrail. He reached over and snatched sets of zip cuffs from Jacob's tactical vest and locked the ends of the chain in place. He tested the stability of the hasty lock and nodded his approval to Murphy.

Murphy turned and, holding his light up the stairwell, slowly patrolled forward. The heavy fire door at the second floor was locked, and one look told them it would be difficult to open with the crowbar. They stood near it, listening but found only silence. They continued up to the next floor, which was also locked. Murphy began to round the corner to enter the landing that brought them to the fourth floor but stopped and stepped back. He pointed ahead to the next floor's fire door—it was slightly ajar.

The sound of a glass bottle being knocked over rattled across a tile floor from above. Jacob crouched and held his breath as the sound of footsteps echoed into the stairwell. Murphy reached his hand forward and clicked off the light. A dim, soft glow emanated from the open door. Murphy knelt down and took a long lunging step round the corner, squaring up on the exit above. Stephens quickly moved forward, grabbing an angle and covering the other soldier from the corner.

"Who's there?" Murphy called out, causing Jacob to flinch with surprise; he hadn't expected the soldier to announce their position like that.

Sounds of scrambling above and muffled voices reached Jacob's ears and the light went out. Jacob clutched the handrail and strained his ears to pick up the sound of Murphy's boot treads slowly ascending the staircase.

"Don't ya'll come up here—I'll blow ya'll back to hell where ya come from!" a woman's voice shouted.

"Now hold up!" Murphy said. "We're not here to hurt anyone!"

"Ya'll ain't dragging me off; you'll have to kill me first!"

Stephens moved up the steps, holding a palm up to Murphy as he passed. Murphy nodded his approval. "What the hell you talking about, lady? We ain't the darkness!"

"The hell you ain't; now get to stepping before I come at you with this twelve gauge!"

"Lady, you ever seen one of those things in an argument?" Stephens said, his voice lower.

After a pause the woman answered, "Well, no, I guess I haven't."

"Ma'am, now I'm coming up; if you shoot me… well, you're gonna have some explaining to do to my momma," Stephens said.

Still staying in the cover of the stairwell, Murphy stepped ahead and followed close behind Stephens while Jacob held back on the rail. He watched as the light came back on and a shadow cut across it. Stephens stepped up the stairwell, the soft light outlining his form as he cautiously took the steps one at a time. Jacob observed as Stephens let go of his rifle and, letting it hang slack from the sling, stepped to the landing at the top of the stairs. He put his hands up and extended them into the hallway.

"Okay, see my hands? I don't intend no harm on y'all. I'm coming in, okay?" Stephens said, speaking calmly.

"Yeah, I see 'um," the woman answered.

"Nana, just put the gun down," a younger man's voice called.

Stephens continued to extend his arms as he walked into the hallway. He stepped clearly into the light and held his hands up, the soft light illuminating his face and uniform. Garbled words were exchanged in soft voices. Then Stephens peered back into the stairwell, looking at Murphy and Jacob, and said, "You can come up." Murphy lowered his weapon and waved Jacob forward.

Chapter 15

An elderly grey-haired woman stood looking at them suspiciously, a shotgun tightly gripped in her hands. A young man walked past her and greeted Stephens enthusiastically. "Good to see you, brother. Where's everyone else? When are we leaving?"

Moving Jacob ahead, Murphy stepped out of the stairwell to stand beside Stephens and looked back into the dark hallway. He tried to close the door behind him but found it was stuck open.

"Mr. Carson broke the door when the elevators went out. Door was locked from the inside, and it was the only way to get back up here," the young man said, watching Murphy's attempts to secure the entrance. "He was supposed to come back for us… but never did."

"What's your name, kid?" Stephens asked.

"Tyree," he answered.

"Tyree, why didn't you all leave with the others?"

The young man placed his hand on the older woman's arm. "Nana, you can go back inside," Tyree whispered.

She looked at the strangers and shook her head at them before turning and walking back down the dark hallway. Near the end of the passage, she stopped and threw them one last scowl before disappearing into an apartment.

The young man looked back at Stephens. "My papa has been ill for a while and he can't walk; he's in a chair and needs oxygen. When the folks came to get us on the bus, they didn't have an ambulance or a wheelchair for him. The police said they'd send someone, but they dint."

"This place was locked up tight. Boarded and chained," Murphy pointed out.

Tyree nodded his head. "That was Mr. Carson, the landlord. He stayed back with my grandparents to help them out after they got everyone else out. Nana and Papa were the only tenants left in the building. He watched over them till me and my cousin got here. Carson locked us in, sealed up the building, and went for help."

"When was this?" Murphy asked.

"Bout three days ago, maybe. After the electricity shut off," Tyree said. "You all thirsty? We got water… food."

"Thank you, I could use a bite. We've been on the move since yesterday," Murphy answered.

An explosion in the distance roared outside and shook the building, causing the windows at the ends of the hallway to rattle. Jacob stepped back and put his hands to the wall.

"It's okay. That shit's happening a lot, but this ol' building is tough; it ain't falling down anytime soon," Tyree said as he turned to walk toward the apartment at the end of the hall.

Stephens glanced over at Murphy. When all Murphy did was shrug his shoulders, Stephens sarcastically smiled before stepping off to follow Tyree. Murphy started to follow as well when Jacob reached out a hand and grabbed his forearm. "What are we doing? We need to keep moving."

"Relax, we're just stopping long enough to get eyes on the area, and we'll be on our way," Murphy said, pulling away and following Stephens.

Jacob stood looking down the dark hallway; every apartment door was partially opened, and the windows at each end of the long hallway had been covered with paper. He turned and glimpsed back at the broken door as explosions outside made an ominous rumbling sound that crept up the stairwell. Listening to the growling echo up the stairs and the trembling as the building protested the concussion of every bomb drop, Jacob suddenly realized he was alone in the dimly lit space. Shaking himself, he quickly moved out after his friends.

Jacob reached the apartment the others had entered and, slipping quietly through the open door, paused in a small hallway. The apartment was neatly made up and well kept. Family pictures covered the walls and Jacob recognized Tyree in several of them—as a young boy sitting on a sailboat and holding a fishing pole, group photos of happier times, but most notably, his high school graduation photo, enlarged and holding a prominent spot above a large maple bench.

Jacob followed the voices he could hear to the end of the small hallway. He walked into a living room where an elderly man, wearing an oxygen mask, lifted a hand to wave. Jacob forced a smile and returned the gesture as younger man, possibly late teens, moved from the kitchen and looked Jacob up and down. "You a cop?" he asked accusingly.

Jacob sighed and shook his head. "You know, I'm going to have to get a new tailor."

"What's that supposed to mean?" the kid asked.

"Means I found this gear in the back of a cop car. I'm not a police officer," Jacob answered.

"Cool, because I got warrants," the kid said.

The old man snapped the oxygen mask from his face, the sudden movement catching Jacob's eye. "James, will you shut up? The police ain't sending nobody out here to arrest you for speeding tickets." The old man looked up at Jacob. "Pardon my grandson; he tries to play tough, but he's harmless."

"Papa, will you stop? We don't owe these folks any explanation," James said, looking embarrassed.

"Child, hush, and go get this fella something to eat," the old man ordered.

Jacob let his arms relax, still not used to the weight of the rifle and tactical vest. Seeing his discomfort, the old man offered him a seat. Jacob moved across the room, pushed aside crumpled blankets and pillows, and sat at the corner of a sofa. He closed his eyes and tipped his head back as the weight relaxed from his back.

"Sorry about the mess; the boys been staying with us and we ain't got a lot of room," the man said.

Jacob scanned the space; it was a humble apartment—heirloom furniture, sofa and chairs, a small dining table for two just outside of the kitchen door. The windows had heavy blankets pulled over them, sealing out the light. The apartment door was open, but Jacob could see where furniture had been pushed against it at one point.

Following Jacob's stare to the front door, the old man said, "We used to keep it closed up but we leave it open 'cause the floor is empty now and the doors downstairs is all locked. Might need to change our policy, though, considering you folks just walked up on us like that."

James returned to the room and eyed Jacob suspiciously before handing him a plate and a small plastic cup. "Here, it's just water and a grilled cheese."

Jacob accepted the plate. "Been a bit since I had a hot meal; thank you."

"I wish I had more for you. Y'all can call me Ernest, or Ernie; most my friends do. Gas is still on up here; keeps the stove going. Some water pressure from the tank on the roof, but not sure how long that'll last."

Jacob took a long drink of the water. He looked at Ernie and nodded. "It's good, thank you, sir."

"Sorry, I didn't catch your name."

"I'm Jacob."

The old man turned his head, stretching to see into the kitchen. "Listen, Jacob, I know what's happening out there. I been hearing what they say on the radio."

Jacob looked to the old man. "I don't have answers, if that's what you're asking—" He stopped as the sound of an explosion rattled the windows and shook the building.

The old man shook his head. "I'm not looking for that, Jacob. I need you to get the boys out of here. I already talked it over with the wife; we won't last out there, especially not on those streets... not in no shelter, either. We'll be okay up here; we got food and water and can get by for some time on our own. I need you to promise that when you leave, you'll take the boys."

Tyree walked into the room. "Papa, I already told you we ain't leaving without you, so stop bothering this man."

"You got to; these folks will need your help, anyhow."

Jacob looked at Tyree and noticed the others were now moving out of the kitchen.

"How, exactly, would we need their help?" Jacob asked.

"They know the streets. You'll find that the roads are all blocked. These two can get you in and out and up to the island—I know that's where you all are headed; no other reason for you to be up this far."

Murphy stepped into the room, raising a hand as he swallowed. "What do you know about the roads being blocked?" Murphy asked. He took a seat next to Jacob, holding a half-eaten sandwich.

Ernie grinned and pulled back a blanket on his lap. He had a small handheld police scanner. He held it up and clicked it on; hearing nothing but static, he powered it back off. "It was alive with reports up till about four hours ago. That's when the fire department called in for help. We heard their distress calls; said they were pulling back to the south. Later, those men out front, they got shot up and their vehicles wrecked.

"That street out front will get you killed. You're gonna have to stick to the alleys. These boys can help you."

Tyree raised his hand and stepped closer to face Ernie, moving behind his chair and leaning over his shoulder. "I told you, Papa, we ain't leaving. Now stop this."

"It's okay, Ty," the old woman said. "Your grandfather and I already discussed it; it's all been figured on. You know I can't go running and jumping over no fences, and no way I'd go an' leave him here alone. When you get to the island, you can tell 'em where we be and they'll come back for us. I got plenty here to take care of your Papa."

Tyree looked down and shook his head, then stepped away while looking toward the hall and staring at the door. James moved from the kitchen and hugged the woman. "Don't make us go, Nana," he said, his voice breaking.

The old man cleared his throat and looked back at Jacob. "Now, you all can take what you need. The boys scrounged up plenty from the empty units, but you need to be going quick. It's been quiet for a couple hours, but you can bet it won't last."

"Wait!" Murphy said loud enough to silence them. "Tell me about what happened out front; you saw it?"

Tyree turned away and looked at Murphy. "I saw it… I was on the roof."

"Who did it, and how?"

"It was a bunch of trucks and a school bus; they was driving down the center of the street, then the people… you know them, the ones on the news—"

"The Darkness," Stephens said.

"Yeah, it was them. They come out and filled the street; they was pushing at the vehicles, you know crowding around them, trying to open the doors to get in. But the trucks didn't stop; they just kept going, slowly pushing them out of the way. Then it was like… shooting from everywhere. The trucks tried to speed up through the crowd, but more of 'em—these different ones with guns—they started shooting. The army guys, they started shooting back.

"Well, one of them things had a bazooka or something because it blew a hole right through one of those tanks out there; the one out front."

Stephens nodded. "Yeah, and then what?"

"Well, mostly the vehicles kept going right through it, leaving that one out front to burn. Later, some helicopters flew by and I waved to them from the roof, but they didn't stop. When I looked back at the street… they was all gone… every last one of 'em.

"I still been seeing them. Right before you showed up, a group moved down the street, all carrying rifles. A woman ran to them for help… they tackled her and drug her off."

"Where did they take her?" Stephens asked.

"I don't know. Just gone… up the street somewhere."

"You think you can get us to Northerly Island through all of that?" Murphy asked.

"No… no way. Not through the city—too many people and too many places for them to get at us. You're talking ten miles on foot. If it was that easy, I would have already tried."

"So think about how you would go now. How would you go if you had to, without being seen?"

"Go to the lake," Nana said.

Murphy looked at her. "Yes, ma'am, that's where we want to get."

"No, I mean straight to the lake; you could go through the Oak Woods Cemetery and then to the harbor," Nana said.

Murphy looked at her, then back to Tyree.

Tyree nodded his head. "She's right. It's only a couple miles if we cut through the graveyard."

Stephens chuckled. "For real man? You want to go through the friggin graveyard? In the middle of the night?"

Murphy put up a hand, silencing Stephens as he got to his feet and stepped toward Tyree. "Take me to the roof and show me the route."

Chapter 16

Jacob followed the others back down the hallway, into the stairwell, and out a roof access door. Jacob used a sleeve to wipe his forehead; it was raining again and hot. The humidity made the air feel heavy and sweat instantly built up under the vest on his back. The rain drizzled in and tapped at the rubber and pea-stone surface of the roof as Tyree led them to the north corner. Just before he reached the end, he crouched low and waited for them to gather around.

"I've seen them down there all around those streets. So watch yourself," Tyree said, before turning back and moving slowly toward the edge. He moved right to the end, and then squatted back on his heels behind a stubbed wall that ran the perimeter of the roof.

Jacob hung back as Murphy scooted next to Tyree and looked out over the edge. "What am I looking at?" he whispered.

Tyree reached into a light backpack he'd carried with him up to the roof and pulled out a red collapsible toy telescope that he handed off to Murphy. Murphy looked at it in his hand. "Really? How old are you, man?"

"Gimme a break, I found it in one of the apartments," Tyree said.

Murphy grinned and extended the scope. He looked out over the edge of the building and down at the dark streets. Jacob watched him scanning from left to right before lowering the scope and looking back. "Okay, again, what am I looking at?"

Tyree pointed in the distance. "See out there at the end of this road—the bridge? We gotta go all the way down this street about five blocks, under the Skyway, and then under the el tracks. After that, we'll get to the cemetery wall; it's about eight feet high. There's lower spots than that, but there's barbed wire at them places."

"Walls and barbed wire? What kind of cemetery is this?" Jacob whispered.

"Come on, man, it's Chicago. Don't act like you never heard of fences to keep folks out," Tyree said.

"Okay… back on topic. What's it look like inside?" Murphy asked.

"It's big, man—like a park; lots of places to hide, trees, and small lakes. A road goes right down the middle, almost all the way to Jackson Park. From there, it's right to the golf course and lakeshore."

Murphy scanned with the scope and handed it off to Stephens, who took his spot near the edge of the roof. Murphy moved away, pulling Tyree with him. "This harbor; you sure there will be boats there?"

Tyree shrugged. "It's a harbor, ain't that where they stay? Summertime, docks should be full this time of year. Papa used to keep a boat there; he used to take us out all the time before he went in the chair and had to sell it. But I ain't exactly been out fishing lately, ya know."

"Okay, so you and your brother, you have weapons?"

Tyree shook his head. "James ain't my brother; he's my cousin… and no, just the pump gun and we can't take that. Nana wouldn't give it to me, anyway."

Jacob reached down and un-holstered his pistol. He looked at Tyree and held it to him. "Take this; I'm no good with it," he said.

Murphy nodded. "Okay, good, but you'll need to find a bat, bar, or whatever; you and your bro— cousin need to be able to fight. Let's get back downstairs. I want to be moving while it's still quiet."

***

The old woman stuffed bags of food and bottles of water into their already over-stuffed backpacks. Jacob looked away while the boys hugged her and promised to return. He didn't want to be torn again by thoughts of his wife and daughter… where they may be, if they made it to the island, were they evacuated, or were they on the bus that was attacked on the road? He wanted to push it out of his mind, but he wasn't trained to act like the soldiers that were guiding him, the ones that could turn off emotion and fight. Jacob tried to mimic them but he failed.

Now there would be another burden on the two men in uniform—civilians like him to slow the soldiers up and possibly cause more problems. Jacob hoped it wouldn't be too much. He watched as Tyree released his grandmother, turned away from her, and used the sleeve of his shirt to wipe away tears.

"It's okay," Stephens whispered to him. "We're gonna send someone back for 'em."

Tyree clenched his jaw and nodded his head before looking away. He reached down and put on his backpack. "I know," he whispered. He stepped off toward the stairwell, leading the way with a small flashlight.

When they reached the bottom of the stairs, Stephens untied the door.

"Dark from here on out; go on and cut that light," Stephens whispered.

After the light was cut, he took the lead position and opened the door to the dark lobby. As Jacob had done before, Tyree kept his hand on Stephens' armor and was led helplessly into the lightless lobby. James did the same, holding Tyree. Murphy gave them a moment to move ahead, then looked back at Jacob. He flashed a thumb up then dropped his goggles and stepped into the dark with Jacob holding his gear.

They moved slowly, but it wasn't graceful or quiet. Jacob heard one of the boys breathing heavily, nearly hyperventilating. Trying to calm him, Stephens whispered, "It's okay, bro, I got you; we're almost out."

Objects were kicked across the floor, causing gasps; their shoes seemed to slap heavily on the tile and bounced eerie echoes off the walls. Murphy suddenly stopped and Jacob bumped into him, his rifle clacking against the back of Murphy's pack. Jacob felt Murphy's gloved hand push him back against a wall. He sensed, and heard, the boys standing next to him. One of them was trembling; his legs were shaking, every movement making a noise. "Just relax, I'm here," Tyree whispered.

"Wait one; we're gonna pop the door, peek outside, and we'll be back for you all," Murphy whispered.

Jacob heard them quickly step away. The door opened and the clang of a chain on the south side rang as it was pulled tight. Jacob could see a faint slice of moonlight cut through the narrow opening in the door. Stephens was kneeling down with the bolt cutters in his hands. He stretched them through the opening and strained to squeeze the arms together; after a loud clang, the chain was cut and fell to the hard concrete.

Slowly, Stephens pushed the door all the way open, walked out, and pressed against it while keeping his rifle up. With the door fully open, blue light spilled into the lobby. The rains had stopped and the sky was clearing, allowing some stars to peek through. He pointed at the men along the wall and signaled for them to move. Jacob reached out a hand

and helped guide James to the door. Two steps in and the boy panicked.

"No, I can't," he said, pushing off violently and sprinting for the stairwell. They could hear his footfalls and the stairwell door fly open and slam shut.

Tyree turned to go after him just as Stephens raised and fired his rifle. The bright muzzle flash filled the void in the lobby. "Leave him! There's no time; move your ass!" Murphy shouted. "Get out here!"

"No, we gotta go back," Tyree yelled.

Murphy grabbed the man by the collar and shoved him forward. "You stay and you'll lead those things back to the building!"

Jacob stepped out, pushing Tyree ahead of him, and Murphy quickly shut the door, shoving hard to feel the lock catch as it closed before he knotted the chain through the handle for extra security. Murphy then slapped Stephens on the back, indicating he was ready to move just as two rounds impacted the building directly above his head. Stephens already had his rifle up and was returning quick-aimed shots of twos while Murphy pushed the others ahead.

Jacob stopped and pivoted while attempting to raise his rifle. Murphy reached out and shoved him forward yelling, "Run!"

Stephens lowered his weapon and cut away at a sprint, catching up fast, already passing Jacob and pulling ahead. Sprinting with his head down, Tyree was close behind him. Jacob ran down the right side of the street, struggling to keep up and feeling the pain in his ribs and hip. Murphy moved alongside him and turned out as Stephens stopped at a street corner, then pressed against a building to look down the street to the left.

Murphy pushed Jacob ahead. "What happened back there?" Murphy whispered.

Stephens briefly looked back over his shoulder. "I saw three of 'em and one had a rifle."

"You sure it was one of them?" Murphy questioned.

"Nope, but I know it wasn't one of us," he answered. "Corners clear. Cover me while I move. Send 'em when I get to the other side."

"Roger; got you covered," Murphy snapped back.

Stephens looked left and right one more time before sprinting to the far side of the street. Murphy waited a count of ten then slapped Tyree to follow. After another brief count, he slapped Jacob.

Jacob ran into the center of the street and nearly fell while clumsily moving forward. Struggling under the weight of the vest, he had to concentrate on his footfalls but felt as if his legs were wobbly, and he would fall at any moment. He ran full speed, stepping up onto the opposing curb. Failing to slow down and not seeing clearly, he lost his footing and slapped face first into the building.

Tyree caught him as he bounced back. Looking around, Jacob felt the sting on his face but shook it off and aimed his rifle out, waiting as he heard Murphy running across the street. Murphy dropped against the wall between them then slapped Stephens on the back and pushed him forward, telling him to move out.

Out of immediate danger now, they walked ahead slowly and hugged the left side of the street. The neighborhood changed to small storefronts, mixed in with the apartment buildings. They crossed another street and fell in alongside a three-story brick building.

Cars were crammed in tight along the fully congested street. Ahead, Jacob could begin to see the Skyway overpass. They paused and knelt to look down at the slowly descending elevation of the street as it dropped under the highway. Jacob strained his eyes trying to see into the dark shadows below the overpass. As he looked, the shadows appeared textured and to have movement. He blinked his eyes and looked away, trying to focus. They appeared like smoke as the shadows moved and twisted to roll in on themselves.

"We have to find another way," Stephens whispered. "I don't wanna go down there."

The smoke moved up the road in their direction. As the mass caught the moonlight, they materialized into a wide-bodied parade of men and women pressing against each other shoulder to shoulder and spreading out as they escaped the confines of the tunnel. As they moved into the light, the mass picked up speed, and like water running from a hose, they spread out and flooded the open ground.

Murphy turned to the building and Jacob followed his gaze; the windows were barred and there was no time to cross the street. Jacob spun to look behind them, at the way they'd come, and saw it would be a long run to the corner to get to any cover. Murphy grabbed Jacob's arm. "No time… into the street," he whispered.

"What? No way!" Tyree said from where he hid behind Stephens.

"Get under the cars. We have to let them move past us," Murphy ordered as he rushed hunched over to the curb. Jacob ran up the street in the direction of the approaching mass, following Murphy. Searching for the right spot, they found a long and wide delivery truck with cars pressed against it on either side. Murphy removed his pack and tossed it under the back bumper before dropping to his belly and low crawling in after it. Jacob followed and did the same, then he felt Tyree and Stephens crawl up close behind him.

Jacob crawled onward, thankful that the vehicle was high enough that he could lift his head. Murphy was nearly to the front of the vehicle, under the engine. He was lying on his back with his rifle on his chest, head to the side. Jacob moved to his heels but stayed on his belly. He laid his head flat against the damp pavement just as the first of the Others moved in alongside the truck.

They didn't shamble along or stagger like drunks; they walked calmly, like mall walkers or pedestrians on a busy sidewalk. They didn't moan or breathe heavy, no talking or simple chatter; just moving one after another to form lines that twisted through the maze of congested cars. They smelled— not like human body odor or retched flesh—but like sulfur, burning rubber, or the fresh spray of a skunk— only sweeter and not so pronounced. It wafted under the truck and surrounded Jacob and Murphy.

Jacob lifted his arm and forced his face into his sleeve. A car alarm far ahead sounded, probably as one of the black-eyes bumped into it. The mass seemed to be stimulated by the noise; their pace picked up and they moved along at a near jog. When they thinned out, stragglers ran to catch up. Jacob looked at the dial on his watch; they'd lain under the truck for nearly twenty minutes—the mass seemed endless. Every time he thought they'd all passed, another group would move out and run to join the others.

After a long bout of silence, Murphy looked back at them. "Wait here," he whispered and quietly rolled to his belly, then crawled forward. He moved out in front of the truck and took a knee. He dropped his hand and signaled for Jacob to join him. Jacob began crawling until he cleared the front bumper. Murphy pointed to a small Volkswagen ahead on the left. Jacob nodded and, staying hunched over, moved beside it to take a kneeling position.

He heard a light clang of metal on metal and froze. Turning his head, he could see that Murphy had heard it too. The soldier dropped and spun on his heels. He lifted his rifle and took a step forward, looking high over a car to their front. Rapid-fire shots rang out and the windshield of the delivery truck exploded.

Murphy returned fire, providing cover while Stephens rolled from under the vehicle and let his weapon join the fight. "Get your rifle up, Jacob!" Murphy said.

Jacob hesitated and looked around, searching for cover, as he witnessed the two soldiers square off to the threat, weapons up, firing, and walking directly into the enemy. Tyree was quickly on his feet and following close behind Stephens, the pistol gripped tight by both hands while he fired ahead. Jacob took a deep breath and stepped off before stopping again. "The bags," he called out, talking about the rucksacks at the back of the truck.

"Move up, dammit!" Murphy ordered. "Leave them!"

Jacob leveled his rifle and fired at the muzzle flashes coming from ahead. The dark space under the bridge lit up like a field of fireflies. Jacob moved straight on, facing them, ducking behind cars, then aiming at the flashes, pulling the trigger, finding a new target, moving, ducking, and firing. While they moved, the fireflies dimmed as their numbers dwindled. Soon, they were at the entrance to the tunnel.

Murphy held up an arm to pause the group before leaning back and resting against a sedan as he changed out the magazine in his rifle. Jacob walked forward and joined him, mimicking Murphy's movements while reloading his own rifle. A body dressed in jeans and a casual T-shirt lay at his feet. The thing was holding a black rifle with a synthetic stock and scope; its black eyes stared up. Murphy kicked it with his boot and said, "Police issue."

As Murphy reached for the weapon, a rushing sound from behind caused him to pause. The crunching of cars and the screaming of the mob in pursuit grew louder. Murphy pulled his knife and crouched low to look under the rear of an abandoned vehicle. He shoved the knife into the car's fuel tank and rocked the blade until fuel poured out onto the street.

"What are you doing?" Jacob asked.

"Giving us some time." He pulled the blade from the tank and tossed a match to the ground, the gasoline whooshing and flashing brightly as it ignited.

"Go, Go, Go!" Murphy cried out, taking off at a sprint and leading the way into the tunnel.

Chapter 17

Fire blazed, casting orange-tinted light over the path ahead. Black smoke boiled and rolled to the roof of the overpass above, catching the top and spilling forward. Jacob could feel the heat at his back. He heard the sounds of tires exploding, windows cracking, and sheet metal buckling under the extreme temperature. He struggled to stay with Murphy who was running, dodging abandoned cars, and leaping hoods like a world-class hurdler. Jacob picked up on the sounds of the mob behind him and the steady rate of gunfire to his front.

Moving through the smoke to the tunnel's exit, he spotted Stephens kneeling against a concrete wall; his rifle was already up taking aimed shots as he attempted to suppress a small group moving toward them. Tyree stood over his shoulder with both arms extended, firing Jacob's pistol. Murphy closed in on the group as the last of the things fell to their fire.

"How much farther is it to the cemetery?" Jacob asked.

"It's just ahead, past the elevated platforms," Tyree said, getting to his feet.

"Good, we need to keep moving; the fire won't hold them. It won't be long before they figure out they can go over the Skyway," Murphy said, moving them out.

The two-lane road ahead was covered with rubble; bits of broken concrete covered the abandoned cars, their windshields broken and pushed in. Buildings on both sides of the road showed damage from the bombing. Murphy marched them ahead, hugging the wall on the left side. Again, the road descended while it moved under the elevated railway tracks. From a distance, the station and platforms appeared abandoned. No trains, no movement. They patrolled through the area and continued on to the empty void where the road opened back into a commercial zone.

They stopped at an empty intersection. Storefronts stood in ruins on all corners, their faces a mess of shattered plate glass windows. Empty teargas canisters and riot gear littered the ground. A knocked-over police barricade explained the lack of abandoned vehicles ahead. The street to the left was scattered with bodies, the buildings pockmarked from gunfire. Murphy surveyed the now empty street before turning back to Tyree. "Where to now?"

"We have to go another block up that way then we'll see the cemetery wall on the other corner, toward the lake," Tyree said, pointing.

In the direction Tyree pointed, gunfire raged, broken only by the sounds of explosions. Occasionally, a group of unknown people would run down the street, traveling right to left toward the heart of the city. A group of attack helicopters flew low over the street, headed west at high speed to approach the city center. Sounds of rockets and heavy machine guns rocked the ground. All the while, human screams mixed with the howling of the Others.

Murphy sat silently looking ahead, concern in his eyes. After a moment, he looked at Tyree. "You sure there isn't another way?"

"If we go around, it'll take us all night and keep us on the streets."

Murphy nodded thoughtfully and turned to Stephens; he spoke so they all could hear. "They're up there. When we hit the wall, we have to get over it fast. We get these two over first, then you, and I'll go last."

Stephens nodded in agreement and flashed a thumbs up as Murphy turned so that he could see into all of their faces. "We have to get to the wall; no stopping… if you go down… get back up." He pointed. "That is the kill box; we can't stay in it!"

He paused as a truck raced down the intersection to the north, the front end swallowed in flames and the bed filled with the Others beating the cab. It continued through the far intersection while racing away from the city.

Jacob looked at the chaos in horror. Sounds of the things behind them grew closer while gunfire and destruction lay ahead. "You sure about all of this?" he gasped.

Murphy shook his head. "This city is lost and we're in the middle of it. We have to get out now or not at all. Hug the storefronts; at the last corner, we sprint for the wall. Stay behind me, shoot anything that isn't us, and do not stop!" He reached out a hand and squeezed Stephens' shoulder before taking off to cross the street, running with his head down and rifle up. He briefly looked left down the near street then pushed ahead, crossing the intersection.

Stephens nudged Jacob in the back and told him to move. Jacob stepped off fast, running to keep pace with the Murphy. Still a hundred yards to the next block, he could already see the orange glow of fires and the blue smoke of gunfire. A pack of the Others cut across the street ahead; three continued across to move deeper into the city, the fourth stopped and looked in Jacob's direction, catching the attention of the fifth.

The pair turned and took a step in Jacob's direction. Before Jacob could call out a warning, Murphy had his rifle in action, firing at the one to the left as it moved toward them. Jacob took a step to the side and used a lamp pole to steady his aim then pulled the trigger and watched the man on the right drop. Jacob hit him in the chest—right where he was aiming. Grinning, he looked to Murphy for recognition. Stephens came up behind and smacked him. "Don't stop running! Go!" he yelled.

Jacob cringed, realizing his error as the first three came back into view. After having seen the fate of their comrades, they charged around the corner. Two shots from Murphy and a stream of three rounds from Stephens cleared the route. Tyree ran ahead and planted himself on the corner. He pointed across the street to a tall, nearly eight-foot high, concrete wall offset from a wide sidewalk. Murphy nodded and rounded the corner. Taking a knee, he fired rapidly, drawing more to his position. "Get them over," he shouted without taking his eye off the sights and the distant targets.

"You heard him… go!" Stephens yelled moving Jacob and Tyree ahead of him.

Jacob took a deep breath and ran into the street. He looked straight ahead to avoid the sight of danger to his left. He crossed the street and, recalling the last incident, deliberately impacted the wall, then turned away as Tyree came up behind. In a flash, Stephens was beside him; he knelt over and cupped his hands and Tyree stepped into the pocket. Grunting, Stephens lifted and nearly tossed Tyree over the top. Rounds impacted on the ground around them, popping as they skipped off the sidewalk.

Ignoring the incoming fire, Stephens again cupped his hands and looked to Jacob, who nodded and put a hand on the soldier's helmet. Another grunt and Jacob was elevated upwards. He grabbed the top of the wall and pulled as Stephens pushed at the soles of his boots. Jacob strained and pulled until he was able to throw his leg over the top of the wall. Now straddling the wall, he looked out and saw a group of three charging from behind. Recognizing the danger, his eyes went wide. He raised his rifle and fired wildly, hitting two of the Others running toward their position. The third continued on and crashed into Stephens.

Jacob twisted on the wall, trying to get a new firing position and lost his balance. He flopped and tumbled off, landing on his head and shoulders into a thicket bush on the other side. In the dark, he couldn't see, but he felt hands grabbing at his clothing. Jacob lashed out with his fists swinging and feet kicking against the hands.

"Dammit! It's me. Stop, you asshole!" he heard Tyree yell.

Jacob pulled back his hands and felt a wrist grip his ankle. He was yanked from the bush, the thorns catching and tearing at his clothing and scratching the skin underneath. He dropped from the bush to land on his face and his mouth grabbed a taste of grass and dirt. He crawled away from the bush and rolled to his back, looking up at the top of the concrete wall.

The top edge seemed to glow and reverberate with the explosions on the other side. A gloved hand reached up and grabbed the edge just before Stephens' helmet came into view. He climbed up and lay flat on the wall, gripping the top edge with his right arm as he dangled over the far side. Jacob watched the man strain as he pulled, and Murphy came into view before clawing and crawling directly over Stephens and tumbling into the same thorn bush. Stephens pushed up off the wall, dropped his legs, then fell the remaining distance to the ground and landed on his feet.

Stephens moved off from the wall and took up a spot a distance away to watch for trouble while Jacob and Tyree pulled Murphy from the bush. Once free of the entanglement, Murphy shook them off and motioned for them to watch the area. Unlike the violent activity on the city side of the wall, the cemetery side was still. They'd dropped in just short of a well-maintained walkway where heavy smoke blanketed the ground, just thin enough to reveal a number of crypts, tombstones, and monuments dotting the wooded terrain.

"We clear?" Murphy whispered as he exchanged magazines in his rifle.

"I can't see shit in this smoke," Stephens called back in a low voice.

"Tyree… which way?" Murphy asked.

Tyree pointed with the pistol. Murphy put down his goggles and scanned the terrain, then lifted them to look at his watch. "Couple hours till dawn; let's get through here while we have cover."

Jacob pulled his rifle in close to the vest and willed himself up to his feet. The gunfire and explosions still echoed off the wall to their backs, and the fires cast an eerie light that made the smoke seem luminescent. The tall tombstones and monuments cast optical illusions as their shadows moved in different directions with the strobes of the explosions. Jacob shivered but knowing he had to stick with the team or he'd never find Laura and Katy, he urged his feet to move.

He cautiously stepped ahead until he was with the rest of the group. Again, Murphy directed Stephens out front and took the open side while keeping Jacob and Tyrell close to the wall on the opposite side.

They moved ahead slowly, creeping through the acrid smoke. Jacob pulled his T-shirt over his mouth and nose to block the stench. Gunfire raged close; the rounds cracked off the walls as aircraft flew over, attacking the city with their payloads.

Murphy called out just above a whisper, "Come on guys. Don't bunch up."

The team intended to stay spread out, but out of fear, they continually grouped back together. Nearly shoulder to shoulder, they patrolled deeper into the graveyard; the dancing shadows and gunshots echoed off the tombstone, making it hard to focus.

They met a blacktop path and quickly crossed it, not wanting to stop in the open. The terrain sloped down on the far side, where it gradually leveled out as it met a small pond. Stephens moved ahead, then suddenly dropped to the ground; without question, the others fell with him. Murphy low crawled past Jacob until he was at Stephens' side. Jacob squinted and strained his eyes to see ahead. Then, with the flash of an explosion, a large crowd of figures were outlined where they gathered around the opposite shore of the pond—hundreds of them standing in a tight cluster.

"What are they doing?" Jacob whispered.

With a focused expression on his face, Murphy didn't answer. Jacob crawled forward with Tyree, toward the high grass and cattails that lined the shore, stopping when they were online with the rest of the team. The more he looked, the more his eyes adjusted to the light and Jacob saw that it wasn't just a mob; all around the edges, there were more solitary figures. Looking closer, their posture revealed that they were armed and appeared to be standing guard over the Others. The group made noise and backed away to create a long opening for a group of men that ran through the gap carrying bodies to the water line.

The unconscious victims were dropped at the bank of the pond and their heads were submerged. All at once, the men huddled in the dark realized what they were seeing. The shoreline was covered with the bodies; only their legs— or just feet in some cases— were exposed. Occasionally, one would kick and spasm, inducing a random hand from the crowd to reach down and pull the body from the water. It would be held upright by the others until it could stand on its own. The newly removed thing would drift away from the pack under the watchful eyes of the sentries, stumbling around drunkenly like a new calf learning to walk.

Jacob watched as the new ones were guided to the outer edges, their stride slowly improving over a short span of time. Then they would move back to the mob and merge with it, becoming lost in the mass. Groups would break off and move away from the mass and out of sight as others returned, carrying more victims. The swarm again opened up to accept them and provided a path to the water line. The cycle continued.

"Fuck me… look at the water," Tyree muttered.

Jacob lowered his view to the dark surface of the pond only feet away. The moon's refection barely broke through the smoke to allow the blue steel ball to reflect light back. The closer they looked, the more the opaque liquid seemed to have motion. It swirled and turned over while the surface remained static. Unlike water, the upper layer appeared thick and dense to resemble the look of oil—the same as the blood spilt from the things on the street.

Stephens picked up a loose branch and pushed it forward into the water, scarring its surface. As he dragged the branch across the top, the scratch seemed to remain and then slowly repair itself. When he removed the stick, the liquid pulled off; like a rod dipped into mercury, the liquid held together and none remained on the branch. Where the surface had been broken, the water suddenly began to bubble— slowly at first, then turning to a boil.

"We should go," Jacob said.

Chapter 18

With their eyes focused on the oily surface of the pond, no one was watching the Others on the far side. Tyree let out a high-pitched yelp as he backpedaled away from the bank. Jacob looked up and saw it too; the entire mob had their heads up, and their dark eyes were looking in the team's direction. The mass hadn't zeroed in on their position, but it sensed them—somehow the mob knew they were there.

Tyree continued to scramble back until he was on his feet and off at a run. Jacob followed him, moving back up the hill and off at a sprint, running away from the pond, desperate to increase separation from the mass. Tyree was out front, breathing hard and oblivious to his surroundings. He ran head on into one of the armed sentry and plowed through it. Both of them crashed to the ground, Tyree rolling headfirst to the grass and the black-eyed man falling back and landing against a tree. Stephens, who was close behind, maintained his course and ran directly at the thing lying dazed against the base of the tree. Like going for a long-distance field goal, he kicked it hard on the side of the head before falling to the ground himself.

Murphy jogged up and stood over the now unconscious thing, stabbing it once at the base of the neck for good measure. When he pulled out the blade he paused, looking confused.

"What is it?" Jacob whispered.

"It's different... harder or something." Murphy grabbed a handful of the thing's shirt and rolled the body. As before, he took his knife and opened the man's arm. Instead of being filled with the black oozing gel, the limb now had thick fibrous flesh that extended bone deep. Murphy removed the blade and pulled at the creature's neck; the same snake-like skin extended up to wrap behind its ears and the forehead was broadened and ridged.

Murphy wiped the blade on the thing's shirt before returning the knife to its scabbard on his belt. Tyree and Stephens got back on their feet and moved closer. "Whatever is in the pond, it's changing them," Murphy whispered.

"Not changing... replacing," Jacob responded.

Tyree turned the man's head to look at the neck while asking, "What do you mean 'replacing'?"

"Like a parasite, or those spiders that lay their eggs in their kills so they can eat them from the inside out. We're just a host for whatever that shit is," Jacob said, pointing at the black goo.

"Then we should stop it—put gas in the pond, set it on fire, or something," Tyree said.

Murphy shook his head. "Wouldn't do any good... not now; these things are everywhere. This can't be the only pond. No... we stick to the plan.

When we get to the lake, we can pass this information up the chain."

The sounds of branches snapping and things passing through trees startled them. "Let's move," Murphy ordered. "And Tyree… slower this time."

Stephens grabbed the younger man. "I got him, Sergeant," he said, directing Tyree to his to his front and then moving them out.

Murphy looked over his shoulder as he turned away from them. "Go on; I'll be right behind you."

Jacob peeled himself from the damp grass and forced his exhausted legs forward. He clutched the rifle in his sweaty palms and listened to the sounds of the Others closing in from behind. Not wanting to lose sight of Tyree and Stephens ahead of him, Jacob moved quicker. Soon they were back at the wall, and they turned alongside it so that they were running parallel to the street. They worked their way north in the direction of the lakeshore while gunfire erupted from behind. It was more sporadic than before— quick shots of one and two rounds with long pauses in between, mixed with the explosive crack of fragmentation grenades.

Ahead of Jacob, Tyree and Stephens picked up the pace as Stephens looked over his shoulder. Jacob saw the look on his face. Stephens' eyes showed fear, his mouth opened wide, and then he turned away and sprinted as the noise from behind got louder and closer. Jacob saw bark explode, wood splinter, and tree leaves rip apart as bullets tore through them.

Murphy overtook Jacob from behind and, breathing hard, said, "Pick up the pace; they're all around us."

Ahead, Stephens and Tyree were stopped near a section of a low four-foot wall. Tyree was pulling back the wire as Stephens snipped it with a small pair of cutters. Tyree dropped the wire and pulled himself up and over the wall while Stephens turned back, firing to cover Murphy and Jacob's approach. The rounds were so close to Jacob's head that he could hear them zip past.

Jacob continued running, aiming for the breach in the wall. He hit it fast; without pausing, he outstretched his arms and thrust himself over the wall. He flew high and clear, sailing over the top edge and crashing hard into the pavement on the other side. Landing in a darkened area, he saw rows of railroad tracks that ran parallel to the wall. Beyond the tracks, he spotted another high fence.

Murphy cleared the wall next, and then turned around to fire over the wall into the mob. "A little help, guys!"

Tyree had his pistol up and was firing over the wall when Jacob scrambled to his feet and fell in behind him. He brought up the rifle and fired until his weapon was dry. He pressed the magazine release button the way Murphy had shown him, then fumbled with his vest for a new one. He gripped the top and slapped it home, pressing the bolt release. Jacob heard the clunk of the rifle and, feeling satisfaction that he'd done it right under fire, he brought up the rifle and squeezed the trigger. Stephens pulled himself over the wall between Tyree and Murphy and then took the loose strands of wire and quickly twisted the ends back together.

The mob hit the wall just as Stephens pulled back his hands. The wire screeched and stretched as the things impacted it and more attempted to climb over them. Jacob stepped back when he spotted a shotgun-wielding, heavyset man with empty eyes trying to scramble over the mob that was pressed against the wall. Jacob leveled his rifle then fired into the man and the Others below him. The pile collapsed, but more quickly filled its place.

Stephens pulled the pin on a grenade and held it up. "Run!" he screamed as he tossed it rows deep into the mob on the far side of the fence.

Following Tyree, Jacob turned and bolted. Rounds zipped past their heads just before the grenade exploded. They were running across rows and rows of railroad tracks that ran into the city. Moving east now, they crossed the last set of tracks and came to the tall wall at the other side. Looking back, Jacob could see the things had already rebounded from the grenade blast and were pouring over the fence to charge toward the tracks.

Just beyond Murphy's reach, the wall had a deep shelf where maintenance workers could shimmy along the top. Murphy boosted Jacob up to where he could reach a high handhold. He held it tight to allow Murphy to climb his back like a ladder. Stephens and Tyree were similarly working together to scale the wall. Once they were all at the top, not wasting time, they dropped into deep brush on the far side. They were in a dark and empty residential area lined with tall duplexes and apartment buildings on both sides.

"It's not far now," Tyree said. "The golf course is just ahead, past that the harbor."

Jacob could see that beyond the low wire fences was a long row of duplexes. Murphy directed them forward and into a backyard behind the duplexes. It was a tight-fit neighborhood where buildings had been built close together with narrow strips of grass and parking structures between them. They now moved quietly, taking their time and trying to catch their breath as they traveled. Jacob focused on controlling his breathing; his heart was racing and sweat ran down his forehead and into in his eyes. He wiped his brow and looked up at Murphy who nodded back at him. Murphy then stopped and knelt down near an overturned trampoline.

He surveyed the backyard while his team rested. Murphy pointed toward an old, weatherworn one-car garage. The structure was pushed back against a clapboard fence; overgrown weeds and grass poked around the edges of the building. Normally not a welcoming spot in anyone's backyard, this morning the forgotten and neglected structure would be a haven.

Murphy patrolled ahead, allowing the men to follow close behind as he guided them into the narrow space between the fence and old garage. He held up a hand to halt them before he crawled to the far end, peeked around it, and then pushed back. He concealed himself in the tall grass so that he was hidden from sight but still could see the approach. Jacob dropped beside Murphy to also be inside the cover of the building. He felt the old, warped wood against his back and, because he could smell the lake now, he knew they were close.

Stephens nestled into a tight spot against the building and he rubbed his belly. "Damn, that enchilada MRE I was saving would be nice right about now."

Jacob looked back at him and whispered, "I'd just like a bottle of that water in my bag."

Tyree pulled a small bottle of water from his knapsack. He twisted off the cap and took a sip before passing the bottle on. Even though his mouth was dry, Jacob sipped sparingly at the precious liquid. He could have all the water he wanted once they reached the lake. His stomach growled; Murphy heard the noise and looked back at him, grinning.

"Me too, brother," Murphy said.

Jacob sat pressed back against the building and listened to the sounds of battle coming from the city center. Like a violent thunderstorm, the air rumbled and cracked while the ground shook with the impacts of faraway bombs. The sky was now filled with smoke as the scent of burning wood and plastic hung heavy in the air. Helicopters flew back and forth over them as the sun broke the horizon.

Jacob closed his eyes and let the warm sun dry his skin. He was exhausted and knew that he might not get another chance to sleep. His mind raced, thinking about Laura and Katy. Where were they? And were they safe? Were they worried about him? Was he doing the right thing? Should he have gone south like the first sergeant warned him? He must have drifted off as the thoughts became just a small part of his nightmares until he was woken by a hand squeezing his shoulder.

He looked up into the sweaty, dirt-streaked face of Tyree. The young man held a finger to his lips. Jacob understood and looked across at Murphy who was now sitting with his knees up, his rifle rested across them, and his eyes to the rifle sights. Straining, Jacob could pick up the sounds of movement. The Others were close—and there were a lot of them. He could smell the burnt rubber and sulfur stench. And the sounds, they didn't sound like crowds of moving people—like a parade, or a crowd in a mall—but more like the rush of flowing water caused by fabric swishing against itself and the gentle plodding of feet against the pavement.

They were still hidden behind the garage—Stephens and Tyree to his left, Murphy just to his right near the fence. In one smooth motion, Murphy rolled to his side and ducked next to Jacob into the concealment of the garage. Moving on his belly, he crawled closer to the men, and then leaned forward.

"The street is packed; they're moving again," Murphy said as he looked back at the fence. He placed his hand on one of the clapboard planks. It was loose and pulled back easily. "As long as they stick to the streets, we can cut through the yards. We're close now."

Stephens nodded and moved next to the fence. Together, Murphy and Stephens quietly slid their hands up the plank, patiently loosening it, one precise pull at a time. Removing planks and setting them aside, they continued the process on two more boards until they created a gap in the fence.

Murphy pointed to Stephens and signaled for him to move out. Stephens quietly unclipped his rifle from his harness and held it through the gap with one arm as he stealthily moved through. After a long minute, Stephens' hand stuck back through the gap to flash thumbs up, then an open palm to wave them on; Tyree went next and then Jacob passed through the gap. Stephens shot Jacob a quick hand signal, positioning him to where he could cover the left. Crouched low and duck walking ahead, Murphy moved in behind him.

Tall multi-family homes filled the lot. A beige stucco building was to their front with windows broken all the way to the roofline, and the front door hung wide open. Murphy moved them through the carport and halted the group beside a row of green overflowing dumpsters. Sprawled out in the grass, only feet away, was the body of a woman, her jacket sleeve torn loose, and Jacob could see she held a small revolver in her hand.

He stared at the back of the woman's head, imagining how she'd gotten there and sad that she had no one to retrieve her body. Looking beyond the dead woman, he saw several more bodies. A barrier stood at the end of the carport: an SUV loaded with belongings. The doors of the vehicle were open to reveal an empty car seat still strapped to the back bench. Removing the woman's pistol and dropping it in a pocket, Stephens scouted ahead to the SUV and searched for water and food. After a cursory check, he looked back, held up empty hands, and then patrolled on, quickly covering the open terrain and pressing against the beige building.

Jacob ran next, covering the space in a few strides and forcing himself not to look at the woman as he ran past her. He fell in behind Stephens and pressed against the building. He and Stephens waited for the rest of them before the team formed back up and pushed ahead along the side of the building while still hiding in the shadows. They avoided views of the street, choosing instead to stay close to the structures and hidden from the windows.

They continued this movement of leapfrogging open spaces, hugging buildings, and resting in the shadows. They paused often to rest while hiding and scanning their surroundings. As they moved deeper into the residential lot, the sounds of the parading mass faded. Stephens led them between two tall stacked condominiums along a narrow sidewalk that led between the buildings and to another parking lot. Jacob slid next to Stephens with Tyree and Murphy at their backs. Looking around the corner, he could see a long, dark street laid out from left to right. Just to the front of them was a sheet metal-roofed carport that served as resident parking for the apartment buildings. Stephens hung at the corner to survey both directions before quickly traversing the gap. He crouched next to a car in a nearly empty covered-parking lot before waving Jacob on.

Jacob sprinted ahead and stopped next to the structure, which was designed to keep the weather off of the cars. It was nothing more than a roof and sheet metal walls that stopped a foot from the ground. With the solid cover, he was able to walk to the edge where Murphy called them. Looking out, Jacob could see they were now at the end of the city block. A gravel drive led away from the structure and into a wide two-lane street. At the end of the street was a wall barrier made of coiled wire and sandbags; military vehicles were parked in the grass and across the corner. The passageway itself was blocked at both ends. The scene of a final stand, weapons and equipment covered the street; bloody drag trails moved over the barriers and down the sidewalks, leaving remnants of clothing.

Beyond the barricade was a fortified corner lot occupied by a commercial bank building. A tattered military tent stood limply beside the bank amid more collapsed and tumbling sandbag structures. A fire truck was parked diagonally across the lot and all the windows in the truck's cab were broken. Murphy slowly moved out of cover and approached the barricade with the team close behind. As he got closer, Jacob could see human bodies hanging in the wire. Beyond the roadblock, a soldier was dead on the ground with his rifle still tight in his hands. Stephens stopped next to the body and removed the rifle. He quickly checked the weapon's action, then inserted a fresh magazine and exchanged the rifle for Tyree's pistol. Jacob stood over the dead soldier, not speaking, then turned away to keep watch while Stephens and Murphy scavenged for equipment.

"It's crazy; they recover their dead. All these bodies are... human," Stephens said.

Jacob turned back. "All of them?"

Murphy was going through the Humvee and pulled a soldier from the turret before removing magazines from the man's load-bearing vest while saying, "I haven't seen one of them yet."

Tyree shook his head. "Why would they take them?"

"Who knows," Murphy answered as large explosions to the west took his attention. "How much farther is it?" he asked Tyree.

"We're close... not far," Tyree said. "The golf course is just across the street, other side of the bank."

Murphy nodded. "Let's move."

Chapter 19

Tall shrubs lined the sidewalk that wound along the bank's perimeter. The shrubs connected with a sandbag wall topped with a single row of razor wire. The long wall shielded the containment area of the parking lot, but a large swath of the wall was knocked down, the bags pushed inward. The ensuing avalanche of bags continued down and through the once finely manicured line of shrubs. The wire over the fallen bags was stretched to the point of snapping, its loose un-coiled ends now lying twisted and mixed with the bags. Jacob and the team lay on their bellies at the mouth of the breach, looking out with Murphy using Tyree's telescope to scout the terrain ahead.

Jacob lay looking at the terrain as Murphy pointed out landmarks. The ground ahead was flat and open for fifty feet with very little cover available from trees. Other buildings and structures were far apart so there would be little available to hide behind. Beyond the initial narrow street, ran a four-lane road with a lone bus stop to one side and then a thin stretch of median grass. Beyond the grass was an access road that curved around and led deeper into the park; they would be out in the open until they hit the golf course. At the edge of the fairway, a row of trees ran parallel to a path that skirted a tall chain-link fence bordering the golf course.

"That path," Tyree pointed far into the distance, "will take us all the way to the boats. The harbor is fenced; I don't know if the gate will be closed, but it ain't high. We can jump it if it is."

Murphy looked out with the scope and pivoted, following the path. Then he handed the scope off to Stephens.

"See any of them?" Jacob asked.

Murphy shook his head. "No, but they'll be there… hiding… waiting."

Stephens collapsed the scope and handed it back to Tyree before pulling his rifle back into his shoulder. "How you want to do this, Sergeant?"

"Tyree, you lead. You run into anything, shoot it in the face. Stephens, we have the flanks; run alongside the fence—it'll keep one side protected—get to the harbor, find something that floats. Jacob, how's the hip?"

"I'll live," Jacob answered.

Murphy smiled. "I hope so. We're running the entire way. One eight-minute mile and we're on the water. Don't stop; we have to stay ahead of them. If we get pinned down, they'll mass on our position. We can't afford to fight our way out of that."

"Got it," Jacob said. The rest nodded their heads.

Murphy pulled back the bolt on his rifle, locking it to the rear. He dropped the magazine and inserted several loose rounds from his pocket to top it off. Jacob watched the veteran soldier push on the rounds, then after reinserting the magazine, let the bolt go forward. Jacob mimicked Murphy's actions and readied his own weapon.

Murphy looked up, grinning. "Good day for a boat trip. Tyree, whenever you're ready," Murphy said.

Tyree crawled forward through the crumbling barrier and rose up, scrambling through and around the wire. Once he reached the street, he looked back to ensure he was being followed. Tyree paused long enough to allow the team to gather around him.

"Okay Ty, find me a boat," Murphy said, slapping him on the back.

Jacob watched as Tyree crawled to the edge of the bags then, without speaking, took off running across the street toward the faraway tree line. He felt Murphy's slap signaling for him to follow. Jacob pulled his rifle flat against his chest and ran, trying to keep pace close behind the younger man. Murphy and Stephens were to his left, running just feet away. He cut across the first street, stepped onto the narrow median, then on to another small blacktop road. Finally running across grass, he was in the park.

Tyree was pulling away, running too fast. A clustered group of figures stood up out of the shade near a patch of trees. Jacob saw them and wanted to shout a warning to Tyree. He willed his legs to move faster and try to catch up. A gunshot shattered the silence. One member of the clustered group had a small pistol in the air and fired in the team's direction as the rest of the Others took chase.

Tyree pivoted and let loose several wildly fired rounds, low and wide, in the direction of the runners. Murphy and Stephens yelled for him to continue on while the two soldiers fired instead. They knocked down the one with the pistol and quickly dropped the rest. Jacob was now running alongside Tyree; he could see another cross street and, at the bottom of a low hill, the harbor was just coming into view.

Tyree raised his hand and pointed at a large group running directly at them from the edges of the park ahead. The group was to the team's left and moving on an angle that would intersect them at the harbor gate.

"I see them; don't stop, get to the boats!" Murphy yelled.

Jacob crossed the street separating the golf course from the park, carrying his rifle in his right hand. He pushed himself on and felt his lungs burning. In his peripheral vision, he saw the swarm rolling in closer with every second and he could hear their cries growing louder. They were behind them now and pursuing from the city. Jacob's adrenaline surged as his vision narrowed to focus on the water in the distance. The harbor was now just ahead, enclosed by a tall, black iron fence. The gate was open and Tyree pushed through as the sounds of Murphy's and Stephens' rifles filled the air.

Jacob ran through the gate and on to a parking lot inside, which paralleled a boardwalk and a number of small docks. The first of the docks held several small boats. Having already crossed the lot and hurdled over a small fence, Tyree was nearing the dock when he stopped and looked back at Jacob.

Jacob waved him on and yelled, "Ready the boat; I'll get the gate!"

A sliding gate, secured with a chain lock, was left gaping in the open position. Jacob used his rifle to shoot at the lock, the third time successfully shattering its mechanism. The lock exploded and fell from the chain. Heaving with his back, Jacob pulled at the gate until it broke free and swung toward the closed position. Jacob left just enough space to allow Murphy and Stephens to squeeze through.

The gunfire put Jacob's attention back to the distance; Murphy and Stephens were behind an abandoned car, firing into the charging mob. Jacob spotted a man far behind the mob, raising a rifle and preparing to fire. Rounds already pinged off the car's hood, dangerously close to Stephens.

Jacob raised his rifle. Eye to the sight, he focused on the far-off target and pulled the trigger. A clear miss—he didn't even see the round impact near the gunman. Using a trick his father taught him years ago when he learned to shoot, he aimed low and watched the rounds splash into the grass to the low right of the target. He adjusted his aim and fired again, this time knocking the man down. With the mob now closing in, Jacob dropped his point of aim and began firing rapidly into the mass.

Murphy and Stephens fell back, firing steadily until they reached the fence. Once they passed through, Jacob slid the gate shut behind them. Stephens removed a D-ring from his vest and placed it on the gate's hasp moments before the mob collided with it. Jacob raised the rifle and shot one point-blank in the face. Even as it fell back, another quickly took its place.

"Go; leave them!" Murphy ordered, already turning to run toward the dock.

Tyree had a small boat untied and was standing on the bow, holding a rope while waiting for Jacob and the rest. Stephens grabbed Jacob by the back of his vest, pulling him along as they ran for the small boat. Jacob moved behind while Murphy leapt over the bow and climbed to the controls. When Jacob neared the bow, Stephens grabbed at Jacob's jacket and pushed him on board. Taking the rope from Tyree, he shoved the boat off the dock and into the water, then jumped aboard as it drifted away.

The boat continued to pull away slowly, gliding through the water as Murphy called out, "I can't start the motor; I got this running off the battery, but we won't have much speed."

A round shattered the small windshield; Stephens spun around, raised his rifle, and squeezed off several shots before being hit in the chest. He fell back, nearly rolling off the deck. Tyree dove, caught his arm, and pulled him back to the center. Jacob brought up his own rifle and aimed at the shoreline. The mob was climbing the iron fence and more were pouring in from the sides farther up the drive. They were ringing the shoreline, yelling and shouting while, beyond the gates, more armed men hid in the shadows and fired at the boat.

Murphy fired quick rounds and then lifted his head to yell at Jacob, "Prioritize your targets! Shoot what's shooting at us."

Jacob saw three men running along the roadway carrying rifles, one leading by several feet. Jacob fired then watched the first one drop and trip up the one that was following close behind. Jacob shifted his point of aim, fired again, and saw another man drop. A round impacted the boat's deck near his knees, causing Jacob to dive over the windscreen and take cover in the cabin. He held the rifle and continued to search and fire at targets while the boat crept along.

They were moving in on a bridge and would have to pass below it before entering the channel that would bring them into Lake Michigan. The surface of the crossing was covered with the Others, arms outstretched, reaching for them. Jacob fired up at their black eyes, taking a strange satisfaction in watching them tumble over the rail and into the water.

"We're fucked!" Stephens called out. Lying back against the cabin with blood spilling from a rip in his vest, he struggled to swap magazines with one hand. He finished the task and brought his rifle back up. "Too many of 'em."

"There!" Tyree screamed, spotting two attack helicopters.

"Stephens, smoke!" Murphy called while watching the Apaches circle around in a search pattern.

Stephens struggled with his left arm to free a smoke canister from his gear. He pulled it free of the pouch and tossed it under handed to Jacob.

"Get it on the bridge!" Murphy yelled.

Jacob held the canister in his right hand and pulled the pin. He threw it as hard as he could, but the grenade hit the bottom deck of the bridge and bounced into the water. Jacob cringed, thinking he'd failed, but then the channel surface erupted and the red smoke boiled out of the water, quickly forming a cloud.

"Stephens, get your strobe on!" Murphy yelled. Reaching to his own collar, he connected a battery to a small device that he then inserted into a carrier on his chest.

The Apache helicopters dipped their noses then circled back around, at first flying away before cutting a high angle into the sky and turning ninety degrees to line up with the bridge. They hovered in the air, rapidly firing rounds that exploded all along the bridge just before rockets screamed from the helicopters and splashed into the banks. The bridge exploded in plumes of yellow flame and black smoke.

The Apaches split apart, strafing opposite sides of the shoreline and clearing the way for Murphy to get back on the throttle and ease the boat through the wreckage of the bridge and into the upper harbor. Jacob saw Murphy yank ignition wires from the battery and short them to the engine. The big outboard roared to life.

"Tyree, steer this hog," Murphy said. Jacob ran to the back deck and helped Murphy lower the heavy outboard engine into the water.

The boat rocketed forward with Murphy manually opening the throttle. Tyree cut the wheel and guided them into the channel. Fire and smoke billowed on both sides of the approach to the lake as the helicopters continued to provide cover while they raced through the channel. The boat jetted a course straight into Lake Michigan and away from land.

Clear of the shore, Murphy dropped the throttle and the engine quickly lulled into an idle as the boat stopped hard in the water and bobbed ahead. Murphy went to Stephens' side and found that he was unconscious. He pulled away the wounded soldier's vest and pressed a dressing against his wound. Jacob looked away and back to the shore, now barely visible in the distance. The engine had died and all they could now hear was the water slapping against the sides of the boat.

Tyree turned around in the captain's chair he'd been occupying and asked, "What do we do now?"

"Come get pressure on this wound," Murphy answered.

Jacob climbed across the deck and held a hand to Stephens' chest where Murphy's had been. Murphy tossed back a seat cover from a bench to reveal a storage area below. Throwing out fishing gear and life jackets, he located a small first-aid kit. He pulled the kit open, dumped its contents onto the deck, then sorted through the items until he found a package of gauze dressing, and went back to Stephens' side. Murphy replaced the soaked field dressing with the new pads and then put Jacob's hands back in place.

"Don't worry, guys, it won't be long now." Murphy said just over the low pitch of a red Coast Guard helicopter flying in their direction.

Chapter 20

The thousand-foot long lake freighter was filled with passengers; every inch of the rusty, red, painted surface was occupied by the city's refugees. The passengers were divided and separated along the decks; families were kept together with single men and women scattered along the port rail. Men in dark-blue utility uniforms walked the passageways, handing out paper cups of water and small sandwiches. Other men carried clipboards while gathering names and family information. Tyree sat across from Jacob, waiting for his turn to speak with the ship's officer. They'd already reported the location of his grandparents to the helicopter crew; the information was recorded, but no promise of rescue could be made.

All of their ammunition had been confiscated by the sailors as soon as they boarded the freighter, but the pair was allowed to keep their weapons. Jacob's police tactical vest still provided him with benefits. When they attempted to separate him from Tyree, Jacob quickly interrupted and said they were traveling together. A crew member at first protested but upon seeing the embroidered badge on his vest, he nodded, apologized, and allowed the men to stay together.

Jacob hadn't seeing Murphy since they had landed and members of the crew quickly ushered him away to rally with other soldiers. Stephens remained on the helicopter and had been sent off to receive treatment for his wounds at a hospital somewhere to the north. The ship was anchored far offshore, in the company of several others just like it. He overheard other men talking about how the flotilla had been out for days. Many of the men complained how this was supposed to have only been a temporary spot, just until the city could be secured. Failing that, they would sail north to islands that were still unaffected by the attacks.

A bearded man carrying a scoped rifle and wearing torn, battered clothing walked across the deck, looking at Jacob's vest. He motioned at a space by the rail and asked if he could sit. Jacob agreed, waving his arm and welcoming the man to drop into the space next to him. The man introduced himself as Michael and said he'd been on the boat for twelve hours—ever since he had been pulled out of the water near Michigan City.

"How are things that way?" Jacob asked him.

The man shrugged and lit a cigarette. "Bout the same, I figure; they're everywhere, multiplying by the hour. I don't think this is something we can fight."

"You come in by helicopter then?"

"Nah, I got a boat," he answered before taking a long drag on the cigarette. "Well… had a boat. The

Coast Guard commandeered it. I was able to get a couple families out… I left a lot behind too."

"I was south of Chicago in the suburbs. I'm trying to get back," Jacob said.

Michael looked at him. "Yeah, I heard you all were planning a counterattack, trying to get a foothold on the city. He with you?" Michael said, pointing down the passageway.

Murphy was walking in his direction with another sailor following close behind him. He stopped just short of Jacob and lowered a hand to help lift him to his feet. "Jacob, you're coming with me. Tyree, the petty officer here will be getting information on the whereabouts of your grandparents. Give them what they need; they can help."

Tyree nodded and shook Murphy's hand, thanking him. "What about Stephens?"

Murphy put his hand on Tyree's shoulder. "He'll be fine; the Coast Guard got him to a military hospital—"

"Do you have any news on my family? Did you tell them what we saw at the graveyard?" Jacob interrupted to ask.

Murphy nodded patiently. "Come on, let's go; you have a lot to hear."

Murphy turned and walked away, keeping Jacob beside him so they wouldn't get separated on the crowded deck. They rounded a corner at the large bridge structure where a pair of guards in digital-blue uniform stood watch. They nodded to Murphy and allowed the two men to pass. Jacob followed Murphy along the structure on the portside and neared a ladder where Jacob grabbed at Murphy's elbow, stopping him.

"So? Where are they?" Jacob asked.

Murphy pulled away. "Just come inside; they'll brief us, and then I can answer your questions."

Jacob stood his ground and put out an arm, blocking Murphy's path to the ladder. "Just tell me. Are they dead?"

Murphy shook his head. "No man, it's not that." Murphy paused, looking around him then pushed Jacob closer to the ladder and out of sight of the guards. "Your family is at the Field Museum. They're calling it the Castle—"

"Then why don't they get them out!" Jacob interrupted again.

"Believe me, they're trying. The Castle is cut off and surrounded now. So far, the walls are holding but it's a desperate situation on the ground. They need help."

Jacob looked at Murphy, confused. "I don't understand; what's going on?"

"Jacob… they need men to assault the beach to take back the island and Grant Park… or at least hold it long enough to get the survivors out. While the beaches are assaulted, the pilots can use the distraction to bring in every available air asset to get the survivors back here."

"Why all the secrecy about Laura and Katy; why didn't you just tell me they were there?"

"The captain didn't want you to know their whereabouts until you volunteered to join the assault," Murphy said, looking Jacob in the eye.

"Me? How? I can't go…" Jacob muttered.

Jacob pointed at the badge on Jacob's chest. "I used this to get you in the door. They're desperate and just stretched too thin, Jacob. Most have already given up on the city; they don't think we have the ground resources to make this happen. Some want us to just pull back and leave the city to its fate."

"I'll go, but… I'm not a soldier, Murphy. Hell, I'm not even a cop."

"I know that," Murphy said. "We've got law enforcement on board. They're going to start hitting up able-bodied civilians until they get a body to every rifle and a seat filled on every boat. If I judged you wrong, I'll understand; but if this assault doesn't succeed… well, you know the score."

"Murphy," Jacob asked, looking at him sincerely, "what about your family?"

"I don't even know, man; I left them alone when I reported to my unit. You know how that worked out," Murphy said shrugging it off and obviously not wanting to talk about it.

Jacob lowered his arm to clear the way for Murphy to proceed.

"You know what, Jacob? If my family is in trouble, I hope there are people like you and me trying to help them."

Murphy took a deep breath and let out a sigh before slapping Jacob on the shoulder. Jacob watched as the soldier turned and moved to the ladder before climbing it to a small landing. Murphy rapped on the door and stepped back as the hatch opened.

"You coming?" Murphy called down to him.

Jacob nodded and ran up the stairs.

***

The duo was greeted at the hatch by another sailor in blue camouflage who led them down a dark ladder to below decks. They entered a passageway that stunk of solvents and fresh paint.

"Watch your step," the sailor said as they passed through another hatch.

The sailor stopped and waited for them to catch up before he opened a door and ushered them in. Murphy led the way and moved into what looked like a small company cafeteria. Even though he'd never personally seen one, Jacob knew it must be the ship's galley; the tables were filled with men in varying uniforms—pilots in flight suits, state troopers, county cops, at least four different blends of camouflage. A tall, old, and leathered man standing at the front, wearing dark-green digital camouflage pointed to a pair of empty seats.

Jacob squeezed through the crowded aisles and picked a spot. He watched as others moved through the hatch and filed into the room. Everyone in the galley sat quietly, looking at the floor or their watches or scribbling aimlessly on notepads. The man in front did a quick head count, then held up four fingers to the sailor at the door. The man opened the door and relayed the message to a guard outside.

"Some things never change. Hurry up and wait," Murphy said under his breath, getting some laughs from others nearby.

There was another knock at the door; the sailor opened it and a group in civilian clothing filed through. Jacob recognized Michael, the man that he'd spoken to earlier. The civilians worked their way through the room and found seats in the back. The man in front did another head count then faced the group.

"Gentlemen, I am Captain Nelson. By now I am sure you have figured out that the world is a shit sandwich and we are all taking a bite. The fifty men in this room—military, law enforcement, veterans, and civilians—along with groups of men scattered among this ragtag flotilla of ships are all that's left in the region. We are all that's left to stand against them.

"A very high-level overview is that the city is lost and the state is lost. Our forces have been pushed back; the lines we thought we held even twenty-four hours ago have now been dissolved." The captain paused and walked across the room to put his hand on a table.

"I know some of you have heard the rumors that we're withdrawing to the north. I'm afraid it's true. In less than 18 hours we will all be moving north to the upper peninsula of Michigan. That being said, we have 18 hours to get the remaining people out of the city; eighteen hours before the Air Force finishes what they started and bombs those things back to hell." The captain stopped talking and looked down at the silent faces at the tables. He looked away and pointed to a young officer in the front row.

"Lieutenant Richards, the floor is yours," he said, stepping to the side and finding a seat in the corner.

A clean-shaven young man dressed in a khaki uniform and carrying a dark, leather folder moved to the front. He dropped the folder on a table and turned around.

The young officer cleared his throat, and then looked nervously at the captain. "This is a classified briefing, sir."

"Lieutenant!" the captain interrupted. "Please continue."

The young officer looked at his notes before looking back up at the men in the crowd. "Under these extenuating circumstances, the captain has ordered me to pass on this information. I would appreciate it if—"

"Lieutenant, keep it moving!" the captain said.

"Yes, sir. Petty officer, please dim the lights."

The lights were lowered and a large map of the earth was projected on the wall. The officer removed a laser pointer from his shirt pocket and shot a line running parallel through Chicago.

"Fourteen days ago, the NASA space weather bureau reported a meteor shower that encompassed the 42nd parallel. What made this event atypical is that it ran a straight, precise line down the 42nd as if deployed from a high Earth orbit. NASA, through radar and satellite analysis, confirmed that neither we nor any allies—or enemy, for that matter—had any birds on that trajectory.

"Six hours after the event, the anomalies began. Data collection now confirms the earliest reports were simultaneously recorded in California, Connecticut, Illinois, Iowa, Massachusetts, Michigan, New York, Pennsylvania, and overseas in Europe and Asia." As the officer spoke, his laser pointer drew a straight line across the world map marking spots as he read them off.

Jacob looked at Murphy. "Is this for real?" he whispered.

"Just listen," Murphy answered, not looking away from the screen.

More sidebars broke out in the room. "Gentleman, hold questions and conversations to the end!" the captain shouted over their voices.

The young officer turned away from the map and looked back at his notes. "Thank you, sir," he said as he flipped pages and looked back at his audience.

"Twelve hours after the event, mass disappearances were reported. Eighteen hours after the event, civil disturbances and riots broke out; at forty-eight hours, we began losing communications with remote areas; by seventy-two hours, the condition had spread one hundred miles north and south of the 42nd."

"Lieutenant, let's skip ahead," the captain said.

Richards leafed through his stack of papers and placed them back in his folder. "Yes, sir; next slide please." The men in the room gasped as a fully dissected naked male body was displayed on the screen. The young officer moved his pointer over the display. "As you can easily see, the anatomy of the aggressor is not human. Next."

A new slide showed the same man, but his chest cavity had been cleared away and the top of its head removed. "As you see on this slide, organs do exist at early stages. Although very rudimentary—and with the exception of the brain, eyes, and some sort of lungs—they are not recognizable. They have no identifiable circulatory or nervous system. They have been replaced by a sort of single-cell caustic gel. The gel consumes the human organs and systems, then uses the energy produced to transform the carrier. At the stage in this photo, the carrier still holds a high percentage of measurable human DNA.

"Gentlemen, what you are seeing is a previously unknown, and most probably alien, parasite. It infests its victims via the eyes, nose, and mouth through direct contact with seeder ponds. We believe that explains the black eyes and mouth of the aggressors. We believe these warm-water ponds were contaminated by the original event, and recreational swimmers were its first victims. Next.

"Again, as you can see on this slide, this male has progressed in the transformation. This male has developed muscle tissue and the organs are now enlarged. You may also notice the texturing of the skin. At this stage, the carrier has less than 20% measurable human DNA. This group is more highly capable and cunning. They have been observed planning and using strategy in attacks. Next.

The room gasped and people began shouting, causing the captain to again get to his feet and silence the crowd. The image on the screen showed a CGI-produced image of a humanoid. It had a pronged reptile-like head, scaled skin, a bold chest, and elongated arms.

"This is an artistic rendering of what we predict the final progression will look like—"

"Bullshit," a man in a state trooper uniform near the back yelled. "You trying to tell us we're being invaded by the Creature from the Black Lagoon?"

"Captain, I don't care what they are; just send me back so I can kill them!" another shouted.

Captain Nelson slammed a hand on a table at the front of the room. "That's enough; turn on the damn lights!" Nelson stood up angrily. "Listen for your name and assignment, and then get your ass on deck to be outfitted and briefed by your squad leaders. We assault at dusk."

Chapter 21

Nervous men stood in long lines and crowded along the back deck of the freighter as squads were divided up, arms were issued, and ammunition handed out. Two tall Marines stood near crates of equipment, pulling men from the line to be fitted with protective armor. Jacob was snatched and, after a quick look-over, his police vest was refitted with a chest rig holding nine thirty-round magazines for his rifle and two fragmentation grenades. The Marine grabbed Jacob by the shoulder and spun him clockwise, pulling on straps and tabs, then applying tape to anything dangling.

The Marine looked Jacob in the eyes. "How's it feel?"

"Heavy," Jacob said.

"Okay, you're good," the Marine said before shoving Jacob back into the line.

Jacob learned the invasion force, even though critically short of men, had plenty of ordnance, most of which was flown in from Reserve and National Guard armories in northern Michigan and Wisconsin. Various sized watercraft were being positioned at the bottom of a long stairwell as cardboard boxes full of uniforms and boots were dumped on the deck. The empty containers were tossed over the side to make room for more.

The men were split into squads then waited in long lines, some at ladders to board the small boats while others were organized and led away to the stern to board helicopters. Jacob looked out over the water at the gathered freighters and ferries. Ships of all shapes and sizes stretched to the horizon while small leisure boats speckled the water, bobbing amongst the larger freighters and transport ships.

Standing at the center of the deck now, Jacob was near the middle of a stack of eleven men who were members of his recently formed squad. He looked around in the chaos; the only familiar part of his assignment was Murphy taking the position of squad leader at the front. Helicopters orbited the flotilla, dropping in to pick up teams, then rejoining the holding pattern above. Jacob stared up at a circling twin rotor helicopter, curious about its destination.

"You don't want to be on them," a soldier in line ahead of Jacob said, noticing his stare. The man was wearing sergeant's stripes and the name Cass was written on the front of his helmet.

Jacob nodded acknowledging the man. "Why's that?"

"Air assault. They are dropping way inland off the beach, right on top of the bastards up near Michigan Avenue, a long ways from where we're going. They'll be elbow deep in the shit before we even hit the beach. Higher ups are hoping to draw the things off of Grant Park and the lakefront so we can safely get ashore," the sergeant said. As he spoke, the man's eyes followed a helicopter making an approach to the rear of the freighter where a tight pack of soldiers were waiting.

"That's insane!" Jacob muttered. "They'll be slaughtered!"

"Them's the breaks," the sergeant said grimly, shaking his head before looking away.

"What about us?" Jacob asked.

"Amphibious landing! We're on the boat teams... going right through the breakwater then slamming into the wall. Hauling ass and digging in near the highway—traditional blocking action against an atypical force. It's good though; we'll have wide fields of fire and good cover over the highway... but all that depends on the air assault boys pulling them off the waterfront."

"This is good?" Jacob asked.

Jacob was nudged from behind as the line moved ahead and snaked around a container. His squad of eleven was moved into an open staging area just shy of the stairs leading to the waterline. Murphy was there going over men's equipment and dividing the group into two halves. Murphy then moved against a container and pointed at a sheet of plywood with a rough map sketched on it.

The map, which had four horizontal lines running across it, was oriented so that the lake was at the bottom; a straight line running along the bottom of the board represented the lakeshore. Above the shoreline was another line designated as the trail. A parallel line marked as the highway was situated over the trail. A shaded area labeled park was sketched in between the highway and a final line near the top of the board. This line was denoted as Michigan Avenue and was marked with an X, along with the words Air Assault. At the far left side of the board, at the end of the shoreline, was a box marked Castle.

"Listen up," Murphy said, pointing at the board. "We will be hitting the shoreline here, just to the right of the museum complex. When you hit the sea wall, move in to the trail and wait for instructions. When everyone is on line we will push forward and dig in on the highway that we'll find to our front.

"The air assault force will be hundreds of meters inland; the Castle will be far down the shoreline to our left. Our objective is to take the beach, drawing the black-eyes to us. We need to hold them as long as possible before pulling back south to the Castle. We have to create a pocket to allow for extraction of the survivors." Murphy turned away to push the soldiers ahead as more in the line tried to take the spot by the board.

Jacob was sent to the right and grouped as A-team. The soldier, Sergeant Cass, was placed in charge of Jacob's team. He moved them out of the line and formed them into a small group.

Murphy handed out a roll of what looked like duct tape to Jacob's team leader and said, "Get this on everyone's back."

"What's it for?" Jacob asked as the soldier spun Jacob around and twisted strips of tape into his gear.

"Reflective tape. So the guys in the sky don't kill us."

"Enough chitchat; finish up with the tape and get on line by the ladder," Murphy said, waving the men back into two lines. "We have two small boats picking us up. A-team, I'll be traveling with you."

A sailor pulled back a gate leading through the rail and onto a rusted stair platform. Jacob looked out over the water; the stairs ran down to the surface where another small platform was attached just above the waves of the lake. Two small cabin cruisers were tied on, swaying and rising with the swells of the freighter. Men dressed in dark navy-blue camouflage and orange life vests were waiting at the bottom.

"I hope you all don't get seasick," the sailor said as he ushered the men onto the stairs.

Jacob gripped the rail, not wanting to let go as fear settled in. He looked back at the man behind him and saw the same look.

"You okay?" Cass asked him.

Jacob took a deep breath and thought of his family trapped on shore. He looked up at the sky and stepped through the gate onto the stairs. "I'm fine."

He grabbed the stair rail and took the steps one at a time, steadying himself against the swaying of the freighter. Murphy was leaning against the ship, talking to them as they descended. Slapping backs and checking gear, he waited for the entire group to reach the bottom before he fell in with them on the platform.

Murphy stepped to the edge of the small landing deck, facing his squad. "There were close to three million people in the city before all of this. We don't know how many made it out, how many are dead, or how many are fucking lizard people now. We messed up early; we didn't know what we were fighting and we went soft on them.

"Not this time! No riot shields, no flex cuffs, no arrests, no rules of engagement. If they run at us, shoot them; if they are on the beach, shoot them. If they have solid-black eyes, shoot them. We need to attract every damn lizard person in the city to our position. It's the only way we get our people back. The only way we get our families evacuated from the Castle. We have to get the landing zones clear so the birds can get in and back out.

"Your team leaders have been picked for a reason; follow them. Now let's get out there and kick some reptile ass!" Murphy shouted, signaling the sailors to begin the boarding of the small boats.

Jacob followed Cass to the right. "Mount up," Cass said.

A sailor pulled the small boat in tight while another grabbed Jacob's arm and helped him onboard. "Don't fall in," the sailor warned. "With all that armor, your ass will sink to the bottom like a brick."

Jacob nodded and nearly tumbled aboard the small Bayliner speedboat. Painted white with red pinstripes, it was no assault craft; the bow was covered with a red liner and had a glass windshield and two captain's chairs in the front. Murphy quickly moved aboard and dropped into the seat on the left, while the rest of the team was ushered and crammed into a U-shaped bench in the back. The passengers' knees and shoulders pressed together in the tight space.

Sitting heavy in the water, the boat was filled and pushed off. The sailor moved away from the side, plopped into the driver's seat, and started the engine. It gurgled to life as the smell of gas and oil mixed with the lake water. Jacob could feel the vibrations under his seat as the sailor moved the motor to reverse. The small boat rose up on a lake swell then drifted back while being pulled away by the engine. The wheel was cut, and they moved alongside the tall freighter. Families looked down at them from the top rail; some waved but most just stared with shocked and scared faces. The sailor slowly opened the throttle, allowing the bow to lift, and they broke away from the freighter on a course to open water.

Black smoke billowed on the horizon over the otherwise clear sky. Small specks ahead quickly transformed into an armada of various boats as they approached. Police boats, Coast Guard patrol boats, cabin cruisers, and speedboats of all make and model were floating together in a packed cluster.

Murphy spun around in his chair and looked at his watch. "Weapons on safe, locked, cocked, and ready to rock; it won't be long now."

Jacob followed Cass's lead as he locked back the bolt on his M4 and fished a magazine from his vest, slapping it home and letting the bolt slam forward.

Murphy grinned watching Jacob. "Might make a soldier out of you yet."

He looked back up at Murphy as boats throughout the formation began beeping and blowing their horns. The sailor upped the throttle of the boat and fell into line with several others. The mass broke from a cluster into a deep formation of several rows.

"Listen up. When you get to the wall, get the hell off this boat, stick with your team leader, listen to his instructions, and do what he says; we fight as a team!" Murphy yelled over the wind and roar of the engines. "Nobody gets left behind. Nobody gets taken! Make damn sure neither you nor your battle buddies are taken alive! Got it?"

"Hooah!" the soldiers replied. Jacob nodded, feeling overwhelmed.

With a feeling of impending doom in his gut, Jacob's legs began to shake and the rifle rattled in his grip. Cold water splashed over the bow, soaking his uniform top. A soldier across from Jacob held a silver cross to his lips, his eyes closed in prayer. With a grin on his face and caressing the grip of his rifle with his gloved hand, the state trooper appeared excited. The air roared as dozens of attack helicopters flew low over the water heading inland. Men in the boats pumped their fists at the gunships. Then another formation of larger helicopters full of air assault troops garnered the same response as they sped by overhead.

The coastline materialized out of the smoky mist. A sortie of fighter aircraft flew parallel to the beach dropping bombs, and a wall of flames erupted within Grant Park. Attack helicopters, looking like swarms of bees from the distance, flew in maintaining a high altitude before stopping to hover just offshore. Volleys of rockets and explosive projectiles were let loose and churned up the ground in the direction of Michigan Avenue, softening the landing zones. The gunships peeled off and orbited as the Black Hawks, Chinooks, and Sea Knights approached the beach from the west before disappearing into the black smoke and fire over the park.

With his thoughts occupied on watching the air assault, Jacob lost track of his own situation. The boat slammed hard in the water, snatching Jacob's attention back to the beach. He glimpsed the passing through the breakwater and the sea wall quickly approaching. Boats bunched together as they breached the breakwater entrance, then spread out to race toward shore, already under fire. The pilot of Jacob's boat cut the wheel hard to line up with a hole between the other boats; he gunned the engine and shot for a section of seawall just in front of Queen's Landing and a large flat concrete dock.

Rounds impacted the water. Men were on the boardwalk and firing at them. "Shit, the air assault didn't work!" someone yelled.

"It's working; we can handle the stragglers. Get ready!" Murphy yelled back.

The boat snaked left and right, bouncing over wakes of the other crafts as rounds smacked the windscreen. Jacob saw other boats hit the seawall and soldiers pouring ashore. "We're going in hot! Hold on!" the sailor at the controls yelled and opened the throttle to the max. Just before hitting the wall, he cut the wheel hard and slammed the throttle forward, forcing the boat into a swift turn and rapid stop. The boat's momentum lifted it from the water and slammed it against the wall.

Cass was knocked back but recovered quickly and tossed a looped line over a cleat. He pulled the line tight, ducking under the cover of the wall. Jacob watched as Cass turned and pointed at him. "Go! What are you waiting for?" Cass yelled.

Jacob stood on wobbly legs; he grabbed the edge of the wall and pulled himself up while being pushed from behind at the same time as others scrambled to leave the boat. Although he stepped high, his boot caught the edge of the sea wall. Forcing everything he had into his leg, he launched himself up and out of the boat. Running ahead, he saw the Others to his front charging toward the men invading the shoreline.

"Get to the trail!" Murphy screamed.

Jacob raised his rifle, firing at the ones directly to his front. He felt the state trooper fall in behind him while another solder fell in to his left.

"Push forward, dammit! Don't stop!" Murphy yelled again.

Taking comfort in the closeness of the rest of the squad, Jacob willed his legs forward. Soon they were all falling in line with each other on the trail, firing to their front as they moved forward.

The black-eyed creatures were cut down as they advanced inland. The squad ran to the short wall lining the highway that outlined the main grounds of the park. The state trooper took a round to the cheekbone; his left hand reached up and touched the wound with a gloved hand. He looked at Jacob and asked, "Is it bad?"

Jacob watched the trooper remove his hand, revealing blood, bone, and ripped flesh that hung off his face. "Fuck yeah, it's bad," Jacob answered.

Cass jumped between them yelling, "Get your rifles back in the fight!"

Cass yanked a bandage off the trooper's belt and wrapped his face and cheek while the trooper returned fire into the remaining creatures. All the teams were ashore and bodies—friend and foe— littered the approach.

As Jacob scanned to the left and right, he saw a sea of rifles pointing over the short wall. The soldiers held fifty feet of open terrain along the highway. The other short wall on the opposite side would have to be crossed to get to them. A pair of creatures charged forward, jumping the far wall and running onto the highway. All along the line, weapons opened up and shredded the beasts as scared defenders fired at anything that moved.

Murphy walked back and forth behind the line of soldiers. Slapping shoulders and encouraging them while also assisting with weapons malfunctions. "Watch your lanes! Conserve your fire!" Murphy yelled up and down the lines.

"What does that mean?" a man yelled in a frustrated voice.

"Shoot what's in front of you, not what's in front of me!" a soldier yelled back sarcastically.

The immediate enemy turned away from the highway and back to the fighting on Michigan Avenue. With the highway and beachfront now clear, Jacob could hear the frantic battle and screaming of the air assault teams. The sky soldiers had done their job pulling the Others off the beaches and luring them to their positions further inland. Now the air assault troops were cut off from the beachfront, overwhelmed and surrounded on Michigan Avenue. Gunships flew in making strafing runs, trying to provide desperate cover.

"The Apaches only have enough fuel and ammo for a couple passes," Cass said to no one in particular. "They'll have to drop back soon."

Jacob sat at the wall, staring into the smoky mist and listening to the battle. Distant screams were mixed with the rapid firing of rifles and machine guns. He knew that when the Others finished with the air assault troops, they would move back to the highway. Explosions ripped across Michigan Avenue and clouds of dark smoke billowed across the grasses of the park, obscuring the view ahead. Bright flashes of light shone through like orange glows of fire as nearby buildings ignited.

Far to the south, Jacob could see the transport helicopters returning. They hovered, then dropped to the roof of the stone-walled "castle". Too far to see individual people, he still knew the assault was working; the aggressors were being pulled off the museum, allowing the helicopters to get in close enough to make extractions. The gunfire to the front gradually picked up, and then slowly declined as the air assault troops were taken out of the fight.

"Get ready, they'll be coming for us now!" someone yelled.

Men to his left and right lay pressed against the wall. Veteran soldiers undid snaps on their vests and readied magazines for quick access; grenades were placed on the tops of the walls. An engineer team bravely ran to the center of the road and placed a hasty line of claymores before bailing back.

A man's hoarse scream came out of the smoke. "Don't shoot, don't shoot!" he yelled as he emerged from the smoke and haze. He leapt over the far wall and tumbled to the street then crawled forward before clawing back to his feet.

"Go! Get out of here… they're coming… there's too many of them!" he yelled as he ran across the highway, breaking through the near wall just feet from Jacob.

The man pulled himself over the wall and scrambled for the boats. A sergeant tackled him and pulled him down behind cover, trying to calm him. Jacob could hear the man screaming, yet not able to make out the words. The mob in the smoke drowned out all other sounds. As they drew closer and the yelling become frenzied, the state trooper to Jacob's left backed away from the wall.

"Fuck it, I didn't sign up for this!" the trooper said, turning away. Cass was behind him and shoved him back into position.

"There is no place to run!" he yelled up and down the line. "Get ready!"

Jacob had flashbacks of watching old movies about forces armed with axes, charging an opposing army who stood behind a shield wall and waited for a tidal wave of death to push against them. British soldiers on line, facing down waves of charging Zulu warriors; every man on the wall had a purpose and together, they were strong. If one man failed and allowed a breach in the shield wall, they all would fall.

The swarm grew louder, their feet beating against the sod and pavement. The smoke hanging over the park appeared to boil from the turbulence of thousands of attackers charging under the haze. The first of them impacted the far wall; the rest were moving so fast they collided and tumbled over it as rapid salvos from the soldiers' rifles cut them down. But another wave was close behind, and they moved the mass forward like a bulldozer shoving them to their deaths at the hands of the soldiers' rifles. The next wave slowed; calculated now, they dropped into cover. While looking for holes and running at angles, they hurdled over the barriers.

Tactics changed again and they massed farther to Jacob's right. Wave after wave launched at the wall before the attacks moved to the middle, and then more to the left. Probing for a weakness, they hit every section. Bodies stacked up on the roadway, hanging lifeless on the far wall, and Jacob continued firing into their rushing bodies and faces. When his weapon would empty, he'd quickly reload. He dropped a magazine in the grass at his feet and when he went to retrieve it, he saw the piles of scattered brass.

"How many more can there be?" a man yelled.

"More than we have ammo for," another answered back.

Jacob's hand slapped his vest at empty ammo pouches. They were right, he'd already expended half his rounds, and the things were still coming. A sniper's bullet caught the man to Jacob's left, his head snapping back as more shots knocked out men to the left and right.

"Sniper!" a sergeant screamed.

Jacob prepared to duck just as another mass hit the walls. In coordination with the sniper's fire, the mass was able to break the wall and move to the center of the road. The claymores exploded, cracking like a bolt of lightning shooting down the length of the highway, covering the pavement in concrete dust and thick smoke. Jacob's ears rang from the overwhelming noise. A hand grabbed him, pulling him off the wall, and then turned him south. He stumbled to his feet but upon seeing others move, he stepped off and jogged with the group.

"We're falling back to the Castle," men yelled as they turned to fall back to the trail and run south to the museum.

His view to the right as he ran to the Castle was obscured in smoke. Ahead, though, he could still see the beacons of the helicopters orbiting and landing on the museum roof in their rescue mission. The trail moved up into an elevated road that overlooked the park, where abandoned sandbag fighting positions were being re-occupied by the withdrawing soldiers. When Cass pulled his team aside, attempting to regroup the fleeing men, Jacob could see the stone steps and structure of the aquarium behind him. The museum itself was still far away, its solid walls standing tall while rings of bodies surrounded it. Sandbags stacked in the first floor windows supported rifle barrels of the helmeted men looking out.

A battle-worn man stomped forward. Jacob immediately recognized him as the captain from the ship. Now wearing green body armor and sporting a large cut across his forehead, he moved out of the crowd. He carried a pistol slack in his right arm as he grabbed Murphy with his left hand, pulling him close. The captain turned and pointed to a position far to the south, away from the reinforced line on the other side of the Castle grounds. Murphy nodded, looked back, and waved a hand at the remnants of his squad to bring them in.

Captain Nelson looked at the weary bunch. "You men! Follow me; we have to support the far flank," he ordered.

"Lead the way, sir!" Sergeant Cass shouted back, answering for the group.

Incoming rounds smacked the sandbag barriers behind them as they moved on. When the roar of the mobs began again, Jacob turned; from the overlook, he could see thousands of charging people moving at the elevated line. Machine guns opened up from the left and right while soldiers launched grenades into the swarm. A mortar crew fell into position and quickly set up their tubes before lobbing high explosive rounds into the mass. Muzzle flashes revealed the positions of the enemy in the far-off tree lines, bushes, and gardens. The enemy shooters were supporting the charging mob with surprisingly accurate fire. Jacob was mesmerized by the chaos of the scene and he stood like a spectator in awe watching the battle.

"Jacob!" Murphy yelled.

Jacob spun around; the rest of the squad was moving out to the south and following the captain. He looked back one more time at the murderous mob, and then turned to follow his squad leader.

Chapter 22

Captain Nelson moved them away from the sandbag defensive wall to farther south on the shoreline and into what could be described as the backyard of the museum. Jacob saw the dead scattered over the grounds; many were dressed in uniform, but several were the dried, shriveled bodies that he knew were the Others. Looking to the right as he followed the squad, he could see the back face of the museum; to his left was a sort of park with small snack bars and the aquarium. The captain led them through the destruction and to another walled barrier that marked the end of the museum grounds. As on the near side, this side was also fortified with bunkers—many that now stood empty.

Jacob could see the beginnings of the famous museum running parallel to the defensive line. The steps were covered in strands of concertina wire; bodies were twisted and tangled in the jumbled coils of wire, piled in excess of ten feet. Looking beyond the far side of the museum building, he saw a tall, battered sandbag and plywood position standing watch over a once grassy approach to the museum grounds. In the distance, Jacob could also see Soldier Field, a large football stadium; the approach was now pockmarked with craters and burnt swaths of grass as scorched bodies lay over what was once a parking lot.

A road that led visitors to the museum park was now filled with blackened skeletons of vehicles.

Hundreds of meters out, an explosion flashed, filling the darkened field with a glimmer of light.

"Anti-personnel mines," a man said from up above.

Jacob looked up at the bunker in front of them. Facing south, the nearly twenty feet long structure guarded the rear and flank of the museum grounds. Made from intertwined double sandbagged walls, it was elevated and built on top of HESCO barriers. Comprised of large wire-reinforced bags filled with gravel, the HESCO barriers were stacked side by side until they formed a foundation for the defensive position that was then built directly on top of it. In order to gain access, a soldier from above dropped down a handmade wooden ladder to the group.

Captain Nelson put a hand on Murphy's shoulder to pull him in. "It's been quiet on this side of the Castle since the beach assault started, but we know the black-eyes will be back. We have to hold the flank while the survivors are airlifted out, and then we'll withdraw from the beach."

Murphy nodded his reply.

Captain Nelson pulled him closer. "Sergeant Murphy, I don't know how to emphasize this. It is imperative that we hold. If we lose this position and get surrounded, we will never leave this park. Everything we fought for tonight will be lost—"

More mines exploded in the distance in ones and twos, then several in rapid succession.

Captain Nelson turned and looked over his shoulder at the blasts in the approach. "We were able to convince the Air Force to scatter AP mines all along this area after we abandoned the stadium. It has slowed them down some, but it hasn't stopped them—"

More explosions, followed by heavy machine gunfire from their rear at the reinforced line, caught the captain's attention; he took a deep breath and looked at Murphy. "Sergeant, hold the flank… nothing gets through."

"How long, sir?" Murphy asked.

Nelson looked at the men around the bunker with a somber expression. "Good luck, Sergeant; take care of your men," he said, turning away.

More AP mines exploded, closer now, and the soldier at the top of the ladder shouted, "You guys need to get up here!"

Sergeant Cass stepped ahead and quickly climbed the rungs. Jacob followed him to the top where they discovered that only four men manned the bunker. Of the four, one had his left arm tied off to his body with bloody bandages, and another's face was bleeding from tiny scratches. Jacob moved deeper into the structure, nearly tripping over a row of blanket-draped bodies.

"Hey, watch yourself," a soldier said, looking up from a radio handset. "We haven't been able to get them out. The living have priority on evac."

Jacob shuddered and quickly walked away to the far side of the bunker. He dropped against the sandbag wall and looked back at the museum. Exhausted, he sat back in the dark, pulling his knees to his chest before leaning his head against the bags. Gunfire rang out from the reinforced line on the other side. Men screamed and machine guns ripped off long bursts. When a flare was launched somewhere over Grant Park, he could see the backlit silhouettes of people moving along the roof of the museum. Helicopters dropped in from high altitude, quickly loading passengers before lifting away and flying back out toward the freighters. Jacob stared at the people in line, imagining that he saw Laura with Katy in her arms.

She looked down at him and smiled. He raised a hand to wave, then watched her turn away to head toward the door of a waiting helicopter. Jacob felt comfort knowing that his family would make it out, even if he didn't.

"Come on, man; wake up," Cass said, slapping him on the cheek.

Jacob looked up at Cass, not realizing he'd drifted asleep. "Sorry," he said.

"Come here, I need to show you something," Cass said.

He dragged Jacob to the furthermost right corner of the bunker. The floor was covered with expended brass, and green boxes of ammunition were stacked against the wall. A machine gun, with a large scope attached to the top, rested on a bi-pod overlooking the approach.

"This is an M240 machine gun. You are now a machine gunner," Cass said, sliding Jacob behind the gun.

"Really easy: pull the handle back, lock it, and let it ride forward. Tray opens like this," Cass explained as he pushed a tab, causing a tray to pop open.

"Grab a belt from a can over here and drop it into the feeder tray—brass to the grass—then close the tray; too easy, right?" Cass said, performing the actions and charging the weapon. "You got that, hero?"

"I'll figure it out," Jacob answered.

"Good, get it figured. This here is your basic night scope; it pretty much sucks, but I need you to keep eyes on the park and kill anything that comes at us. If it gets crazy and you can't see through the scope, look over it and walk your rounds in with the tracers."

Cass made a fist, slugged Jacob on the chest, and waited for him to put the weapon's stock into his shoulder before walking away to position the rest of the squad. Jacob tried to get comfortable. The weapon was at just below his armpits when standing. If he stood with his legs apart and leaned forward then the scope lined right up with his eye.

Jacob looked through the cupped eyepiece and saw a grainy image flecked in green and white. He blinked his eye and moved his head away, trying to focus. Moving closer to the eyecup, he clenched his eyes tight then slowly opened them, trying to adjust to the image. He swung the weapon left and right and was slowly able to make out objects. He saw a flash far off from an exploding mine and moved the barrel in that direction.

Burning debris flickered in the scope—the remains of a taxi cab. Jacob swung to the left then paused to stare at what looked like the hulk of a tree trunk. He tried to focus on the grainy image when he detected movement from the corner of his sight picture. A single man, lit in tones of black and green was walking in the direction of the bunker.

"I see something!" Jacob yelled over the sounds of the fighting behind them.

The man continued walking toward him and as he drew closer, more walking figures materialized into the image of the scope.

"Sergeant Cass, I see them!" Jacob yelled again, not getting an answer.

In the scope, he watched the man transition from a walk to a jog; the group behind began running as well and soon the scope was filled with a mass of running figures. Mines began exploding, and the machine gun on the opposite end opened up. Jacob watched tracers cut through the image and when his own finger finally found the trigger, he pulled. He fired a long burst, losing the enemy group as the weapon jumped under its recoil. Jacob looked over the machine gun's scope just before someone in the bunker launched a flare.

The light under the parachute now exposed the hidden creatures. The field was full of them; Jacob pulled the trigger again, walking the tracers through the ranks of charging men. Jacob watched a man in the mass pause and raise a rifle. Before the thing could fire, he was cut down.

"Focus on the runners; we got the shooters!" Murphy yelled, standing beside Jacob and firing his rifle while searching the crowd. "Get back on the trigger, keep pouring it on!"

Jacob swept the gun left and right, the 7.62 rounds chewing through the charging mass. Incoming rounds splattered the sand in front of and next to the gun; even through heavy fire, the mass was closing on them. Jacob pulled the trigger. Getting no response, he looked to the left and found the belt had been expended and the gun was empty. He popped open the tray as instructed, fumbled with the belted ammunition, slapped the tray closed, and racked the bolt. Leveling his aim on a group closing the distance on him, he pulled the trigger. Nothing happened. Jacob felt panic burning. He pulled the handle and racked the bolt again.

"Get that gun up!" a soldier yelled from down the line.

Murphy looked over at Jacob and jumped to the weapon, knocking Jacob out of the way. He pulled the handle back and lifted the tray cover. "What the fuck? Links on top!" He flipped the belt, fixing the mis-feed and slammed the tray closed. "Fire!"

Jacob leaned back behind the weapon and squeezed the trigger; the mob had closed to within fifty feet while he was screwing with the gun. He strafed the area to his front, moving left to right and felt the impact as the mob closed and slammed against the HESCO barrier below. They screamed while trying to climb the barriers to get at the men above.

"Frag out," a soldier yelled, dropping a grenade over the wall, the blast thumping the bunker. More grenades were dropped over the side and Jacob saw that an entire case of them was at his feet, the cardboard tubes discarded all over the floor. Jacob continued to fire as Murphy lobbed grenades. He lost his breath and felt fire in his ribs as he was knocked to the bunker floor. Murphy ignored him and jumped on the M240, getting the gun back in action.

Jacob bit the fingers of his glove to remove it and slipped his hand into the front of his vest, wincing with pain. Expecting blood, he pulled out his hand and found it dry. He slapped the front of his tactical vest and found the hole where the round slapped against the plate. Jacob tried to stand but stopped to look at the roof of the museum—it was empty; there was no movement. Searching the museum grounds behind them, he saw the soldiers were pulling back and running toward boats waiting in the harbor.

"Everyone is leaving," Jacob said, not being heard over the gunfire.

He rolled to a knee, pulling himself up the wall next to Murphy who was frantically working the machine gun, trying to push back the overwhelming mass hoarded around the tower.

"They're leaving us!" Jacob yelled.

"Get on your weapon!" Murphy screamed, grabbing Jacob by the arm and shoving him toward the firing ports. He stumbled forward, hitting the bag wall and looked down into the faces of the screaming mass. Jacob stepped back and again felt Murphy's shove. "If you ever want to get out of here, kill them!" he ordered.

Jacob raised his rifle up over the edge and fired at a steep angle down into the mass. No need to aim; they were so close and pressed together that every shot was a hit. The soldier on the radio lifted his head to yell down both sides of the bunker. "I have two birds inbound! Danger close!"

Jacob dropped his magazine, reloaded, and leaned back over the wall, firing at the black eyes of the mob. Rounds impacted the bags to his left and front.

"Willy Pete out!" Sergeant Cass yelled.

Jacob watched as Cass tossed a grenade into the crowd; it popped and threw white-hot burning shards that ignited clothing and billowed clouds of acrid smoke that blocked the view of the enemy shooters.

A roar ripped through the sky as two long-winged aircraft cut overhead then peeled off, heading north on Michigan Avenue, doing a flyby over Soldier Field.

"Those are our A10s! Here they come!" the radio operator cheered.

The Warthogs looped back around and lined up for a run. The sky roared with the thunder of the planes' cannons firing rounds that exploded and ripped the earth apart. The sound echoed across the park like the ground was being unzipped as a line of destruction was painted to within fifty meters of the bunker, erasing everything in its path. Jacob was lifted off his feet and tossed to the back wall with the rumble of the earth.

The operator yelled down the bunker, "They are coming in hot with Mark 84s—danger close! Danger close! Get your heads down!"

The A10s cut away and climbed for altitude then dove in, releasing their bombs. The sky flashed white and the earth rolled up like God shaking out a carpet; sandbags buckled and collapsed back onto the parking lot below. Jacob felt the floor give as the shockwave pushed the bunker off the HESCOs. He pulled his arms in and curled into a ball when debris and bodies fell all around him as they were being dumped in a waterfall of wreckage. Jacob landed on his belly, debris covering his back; he crawled away from the bunker and rolled into the street. His ears ringing and his nose bleeding, he coughed dirt and gagged because his mouth was too dry with suet and dust to be able swallow.

Jacob saw a rifle next to him; he grabbed it and used it to push himself up. He then struggled to his feet and staggered ahead, only getting a few steps before falling against a bullet-riddled car. With his left hand, he opened his tactical vest, wincing at what felt like a thousand broken ribs. He turned and sat on the hood of the car, every breath bringing spasms of pain. Fires burned all around him and, having collapsed, the bunker was gone. Nothing moved and he could find none of his squad.

He stumbled forward only to trip over a man's legs. Jacob hit the ground with a painful thud but quickly climbed back to a knee as he felt the man's hand grab his ankle. Jacob looked back into the creature's black eyes flaring with hatred. Jacob gripped his rifle and thrust, hitting it in the face. The thing's head snapped back, and then it reared forward to grab at Jacob's feet again. Gasping, Jacob fell to his knees and rolled to the side. Grabbing a broken piece of concrete and swinging, he bashed it in the face. Jacob felt the skull crush his own fingers between bone and stone as the oily blood splattered on his face.

He turned again and fell to his belly. Taking shallow breaths, trying to avoid the pain his ribs, Jacob crawled back toward the bunker. He pulled himself back to his feet using a post and, one loose step at a time, Jacob made it back to the fighting position. An arm moved from under the debris. Jacob grabbed the hand, tugged, and got a yelp in response. When he dug away the bags and dirt, he found the twisted face of Murphy. Jacob dug him out further and grabbed the collar of his armor, dragging him clear of the rubble. Murphy moaned and pushed him off before reaching down to open his body armor and shrug out of it. He reached into a pouch on his chest and fumbled with what looked like a small flashlight. He pressed a switch and stuck it into Jacob's hand.

"It's a strobe; get it someplace high!" he mumbled.

"Okay," Jacob said and nodded. Turning back, he stumbled ahead to a long strand of rope that was tied to a barrier. Jacob cut the rope free and tied one end to the strobe. He moved to a burnt, leafless tree and grabbed a branch; pulling himself up, he climbed until he was as high as he could get, then tied the strobe to a branch. Jacob dropped back to the ground and staggered to the bunker. He could see the things were moving again—not focused on his location, but milling about.

Helicopters flew far off over the city and he could hear the sound of boats in the harbor. Jacob moved back to Murphy's side and dropped in beside him. As the things moved in closer, he readied his rifle for a final fight.

"Don't... it'll make it worse... leave me; get to the water," Murphy said in slurred words, bloody foam gathering at the corners of his lips.

Feeling strangely calm, ready to accept his fate, Jacob shook his head and pulled Murphy to his lap. He watched a flashing light high in the skyline make an abrupt turn; it moved around before it angled toward them, coming swiftly in their direction. Jacob pulled Murphy's vest with the reflective tape on the back over to face them and set it on his friend's lap. He cupped Murphy's head with his left hand, feeling his friend's labored breathing. Jacob was tired; he just wanted to rest. He watched the slow-moving flashing light draw closer.

"Hold on, Murphy; they're coming," Jacob said.

Chapter 23

"Daddy!" a young girl yelled, waking him. He saw her running, her feet slapping the polished tile floor.

Katy easily scaled the hospital bed and thumped onto Jacob's chest to embrace him. Jacob winced and smiled at the same time, hugging her with both arms while a tear formed in his eye. Laura came next, reaching down and locking them both in tight hugs. Jacob grunted and struggled to sit. A nurse in camouflage scrubs scrambled around the bed.

"No, you don't, Mr. Anderson. We worked too hard to keep that lung from collapsing; I'll let the hugs slide, but that's it," she barked.

"Lung?" Jacob said, finding his breath.

"You had significant internal injuries; you need to rest," she said while scribbling on his chart. "Not too long, okay, hun?" the nurse said to Laura as she left the room.

Jacob looked around, confused by the surroundings. "Where are we, is this Chicago?"

"No, Jacob. We're in Canada," Laura said. "In a military hospital."

"Canada... how? I don't understand... how did I get here?"

"They found you unconscious and they brought you here. Your friend, the soldier, helped to find us in the camps and had us brought here while you were still in surgery."

Jacob's eyes widened with recognition. "Sergeant Murphy? He's here?"

"No, his name wasn't Murphy. It was Corporal Stephens," she said. "The Canadians took us in, Jacob. The camps were horrible; they had nothing—no water, no food, and there were so many people there. I thought we would never—"

"Why were you in Canada?"

"The Canadian Army is holding them off and trying to keep them at the borders."

Jacob grew frustrated with so many thoughts filling his head at once. "Where is the man I was with?"

"I don't know; you were alone when I got here." Laura shook her head. "Jacob, we're lucky to be here."

He tried to speak and began coughing; he felt the pain in his ribs as he concentrated on breathing.

Laura frowned and used a pitcher to pour a glass of water. She passed it to Jacob who took it and drank thirstily. "The doctor says you need to rest," she said, helping him sip from the glass.

A knock at the open door turned their heads. A tall black man in a green hospital robe and pushing an IV cart looked in, grinning.

"Damn man, still on your ass… oops, sorry. Pardon my language, ma'am," Stephens said, catching himself. "I didn't see the little one all cuddled up with her daddy there."

Laura smiled at him.

Jacob laughed painfully. "Good to see you… Is Murphy here too?" he asked.

"Jacob… Murphy didn't make it," Stephens said, walking to a chair in the corner of the room and sitting heavily.

Jacob's jaw dropped as he lay back in the bed, feeling his body become numb with shock. Katy crawled higher on him and laid her head against his chest. He lifted his hand and stroked her hair, fighting back tears while not knowing why he was so upset over a man he barely knew.

Laura grabbed his hand and whispered, "Who was he?"

"He was my friend," Jacob said with shock in his voice.

Stephens looked at him sympathetically. "Man… I'm sorry, Jacob; I thought you knew." Stephens turned to Laura. "Ma'am, I hate to ask this right now, but could we have a moment? I promise I wouldn't ask if it wasn't important."

"I can appreciate that, Corporal Stephens, but we—"

Jacob put up a hand. "It's okay, Laura; it'll just be a minute," he said. "I'm not going anywhere."

Laura shot Stephens an exaggerated cold stare before she leaned over to kiss Jacob. "Come on, Katy. Let's see if they are serving lunch yet." She retrieved Katy and left the room, leaving the door slightly ajar.

Jacob pressed a button, raising the back of the bed so that he was nearly upright. He grunted trying to adjust his pillow. "What is it?

Stephens pulled his chair close. "Bro, when I saw you come off that Medevac, Murphy was with you. They tried to save him but it was just too much."

Jacob chewed his lower lip, not speaking. Stephens looked at the door and sat back in the chair. "I told the doctors about your family; they used the Red Cross to locate them and get 'em here."

Jacob forced a smile. "Thank you. That means a lot to me."

"But that's the thing. This is a military hospital. I told them you were part of Second Squad, Jacob. It was the only way I could get them here to you.'

"You what?"

"Our forces are so jacked up right now, they don't know up from down. They didn't question it. I just had to lie, man. I didn't want your family out there in one of those camps when you woke up."

"Is your family here too?"

Stephens looked away then back at Jacob. "I don't know where they are. Last word I got, they were moving them south someplace toward Atlanta, maybe Fort Benning. I don't know. Contact's been cut."

"I'm sorry, Stephens," Jacob said just above a whisper.

Stephens shook it off. "Don't be sorry, bro. I know they're okay; I can feel it. Listen, Jacob, we need to talk, man; everything is gone now. We got pushed back across the border and refugees are pouring across faster than the Canuks can find room for them. The United States south of Milwaukee is lost and The Darkness is spreading down into Central and South America. They thrive in warm weather. Europe is the same way, cold areas are stable while they move and spread south.

"Those ponds we found? They use them to breed and multiply. Most of the dumb ones stay close to their little birthing ponds, but the stage three types... hell, they've been spotted way far north."

"Stage three?" Jacob asked.

"That's what they're calling the smart ones, the ones that shoot back. The fully evolved ones."

Jacob nodded his head, remembering the briefing about the lizard men.

"So what's next?" Jacob asked. "Where do we go from here?"

"That's why I needed to talk to you. I got your family in here, but for them to stay, you're gonna have to enlist—and I mean for real. This base is only for military families. I listed you as a private with

Second Squad. I don't know if that's gonna last or not. You better hope it does, 'cause if it don't, they gonna send your wife and daughter out to the camps. You too probably, once you get healed up enough to walk. There just isn't room on base for everyone."

"I can't leave them again," Jacob said.

"It's going to happen. You need to heal up and go back with us if you want to keep them safe. The generals say we won't last two winters if we can't push them out; we can't survive this far north. We'll all starve."

"So I have a choice of leaving my family to go fight, or leave with my family for these camps?"

Stephens shook his head, frowning. "The choice is yours, Jacob."

Thank you for reading.

I hope you enjoyed *The Darkness,* and would consider leaving a review.
The Darkness
By. WJ Lundy

Other works by W.J.Lundy

Whiskey Tango Foxtrot Series.

Escaping the Dead

Tales of the Forgotten

Only the Dead Live Forever

Walking in the Shadow of Death

Something to Fight For

OTHER AUTHORS UNDER THE SHIELD OF

DEAD ISLAND: Operation Zulu
Ten years after the world was nearly brought to its knees by a
zombie Armageddon, there is a race for the antidote! On a
remote Caribbean island, surrounded by a horde of hungry living
dead, a team of American and Australian commandos must
rescue the Antidotes' scientist. Filled with zombies, guns,
Russian bad guys, shady government types, serial killers and
elevator muzak. Dead Island is an action packed blood soaked
horror adventure.
Allen Gamboa

INVASION OF THE DEAD SERIES
On the east coast of Australia, five friends returning from a
month-long camping trip slowly discover that a virus has swept
through much of the country. What greets them in a gradual
revelation is an enemy beyond compare. Armed with dwindling
ammunition, the friends must overcome their disagreements,
utilize their individual skills, and face unimaginable horrors as
they battle to reach their hometown and make sense of life in the
new world.
Owen Baillie

SIXTH CYCLE
Nuclear war has destroyed human civilization.
Captain Jake Phillips wakes into a dangerous new world, where
he finds the remaining fragments of the population living in a
series of strongholds, connected across the country. Uneasy

alliances have maintained their safety, but things are about to change. -- **Discovery leads to danger.** -- Skye Reed, a tracker from the Omega stronghold, uncovers a threat that could spell the end for their fragile society. With friends and enemies revealing truths about the past, she will need to decide who to trust. -- **Sixth Cycle** is a gritty post-apocalyptic story of survival and adventure.

Darren Wearmouth ~ Carl Sinclair

SPLINTER

For close to a thousand years they waited, waited for the old knowledge to fade away into the mists of myth. They waited for a re-birth of the time of legend for the time when demons ruled and man was the fodder upon which they fed. They waited for the time when the old gods die and something new was anxious to take their place. **A young couple was all that stood between humanity and annihilation**. Ill equipped and shocked by the horrors thrust upon them they would fight in the only way they knew how, tooth and nail. Would they be enough to prevent the creation of the feasting hordes? Were they alone able to stand against evil banished from hell? **Would the horsemen ride when humanity failed?** The earth would rue the day a splinter group set up shop in Cold Spring.

H. J. Harry

NEW REALITY

When the Rixon Corporation released **New Reality**, a fully immersive, five-dimensional entertainment experience, everyone logged on---everyone except Jake and Tom. **As the population gave in to the ultimate experience**, it didn't take long for the world to crumble into ruin. **Facing the wrath** of Rixon and starvation, the pair face a fight for survival and freedom.

Michael Robertson

5/25

Made in the USA
Middletown, DE
14 May 2015